Red Nova

by

Prudence MacLeod

RED NOVA

First edition. December 10, 2023.

Copyright © 2023 Prudence MacLeod.

ISBN: 978-1927478417

Written by Prudence MacLeod.

The days of fracture and bitter loss were destined. It began with the creation of the Gap. The two most powerful witches in history defeated the armada of the Iron Emperor, but in so doing they created a region of space that did not always conform to accepted standards of behavior. To protect his people, Micha led the Novans into the Gap and claimed it for their territory.

During those early days, Micha's daughter was taken, made slave, tortured, and raped. Her bonded companion, Deann, took command of her lover's ship and retrieved her, and for a while all was well ... and then the great ship appeared.

The Great Ship

Michella struggled to sit up on the bed. She found the captain's cabin a bit small these days and quietly wished she'd stayed on Vakay until after the baby was born. No, dammit, he would be a nomad, best he be born aboard a ship. Her ship. "Help me up."

"Sure," replied Deann, offering her hands for Michella to grasp. She pulled the pregnant woman to her feet easily.

Michella stepped closer and pulled her lover to her. "Dee, please tell me what's eating at you. I hate this distance that's come between us. Please talk to me."

"It's nothing," replied Deann, as she turned and started to step away.

Michella held her fast. "That's skeet and you know it. Now enough of this. It's been going on for months. Tell me what's wrong."

"Fine, I will." Deann had spun back to go nose to nose with Michella, fire in her eyes. She placed a hand on Chella's swollen belly. "That's what's wrong. We once agreed we would each bear a child of our combined DNA just like Lady Arlessa and Brenna. You were taken, went through hell, raped, and impregnated. I went through hell to get you back. Now you insist on bearing that thing inside you, knowing what its father was, what he did to you. I don't understand, Chella. I just don't understand."

Michella didn't respond to Deann's anger. "My love, I'm so sorry you've been hurt by this. I wish you had told me sooner. Dee, I love you to distraction, you know that. I want to bear your children, not just one, but several. This one, however, is an innocent. Yes, his father was a right evil bastard and I killed him for what he did to me, but this child

2

isn't him. Dee, that whole experience was evil, all of it, and it haunts me still.

"This child will be born with the Novan marks. He'll be raised Novan; he'll be Novan. He isn't his father. Dee, this is the only bright spot in that whole experience. A baby is a beautiful thing, you've said so yourself many times. I want to bear the child so something beautiful will come out of what I went through. That's why."

Deann's anger and hurt melted away. "Chella, I'm sorry. I wish you'd told me sooner. Maybe you're right about this, a child is a blessing. No matter what else his father was, he was a smart man."

"I wish I'd known how much this was hurting you, Dee. I honestly had no idea. You know I'm still a bit messed up by it and I get a bit lost at times ..."

She got no further. The klaxon blared then Old Rath's voice barked over the ship wide. "Battle stations. Battle stations. Captain to the bridge. Repeat, captain to the bridge."

Deann tried to help Michella, but Chella pushed her ahead. "Go, go, I'll get there as soon as I can. Go!"

Deann sprinted away, leaving the door open behind her. She came pounding onto the bridge and threw herself into the captain's chair. "Report!"

"We've sighted a ship, Captain," replied Old Rath. He was grinning at his protege. "Damn thing is half the size of a planet."

"Hail it."

"Trying," said young Bim. "No response. Captain, there's some sort of energy field around that thing. I'm not sure if our hails are getting through."

"Sensors?"

"Nothing, Captain," replied a woman's voice. "It's not moving. It's just sitting there like a dead duck."

Michella stopped at the door of the bridge and watched, a smile of delight on her face. Deann would play second fiddle, but give her an emergency and she took over like she was born to it. How Michella did love that girl. "Hey there."

Deann hopped out of the chair. "We've got an intruder, Chella. We think it's a derelict, but not sure yet. No response to our hails and it's not moving."

"Huh. You deal with it, sweetie. I'm not feeling so good. I'm going to wander off to the infirmary and see 'Lore. She must have something vile tasting that'll fix me up."

"Need a hand?"

"No, I'm good. You deal with the intruder, and I'll go visit my sister." She turned and waddled away.

Deann turned to Old Rathbone. "What just happened?"

"You just got promoted, Captain Deann."

"Great." Deann sighed then resumed the chair. "Okay, people. We've got a quiet intruder. It's big enough to be a moon and it's blocking the way. Opinions? Options?"

"Personally, I'd like to take a look at her up close," grinned Hawk.

"First man?"

"I agree with Hawk, but I wouldn't send him over."

"Hey now," said Hawk, as he rose from his seat at the weapons station. "Care to explain that?"

"I'm first man," grinned the old fellow. "I don't have to explain a damn thing to you. Captain Deann, shall I explain my reasoning?"

"Please do," grinned Deann.

"Hawk's the best gunner we've got. If that thing suddenly comes to life ..."

"Yeah," grumbled Hawk, "that plus I can contact the king and get an Arcalian Fleet here two weeks faster than anybody else."

"That had crossed my mind," said Rathbone.

"Okay, so we're agreed somebody has to take a look at that thing, yes?" asked Deann. They nodded their agreement. "All right then, I'll go."

"The captain belongs on the bridge," said Old Rath.

"I'm expendable," replied Deann. "The true captain is in the infirmary, still very much alive. I'll go. Comms, ship wide."

"Comms, aye. Ship wide ready, Captain." Bim was grinning. He loved being on the bridge and being a part of the crew. Deann returned his smile.

"Attention, all hands. We've encountered what appears to be a derelict ship. It's the size of a moon. I'm going over for a look. Pally, Barah, Alise, and Nellie, you're with me. Pally, prep our best fighter and make sure she's loaded for war."

Old Rath gave Deann a questioning look. She relented. "Chella's here, so I'm expendable. That ship is an unknown, so I want an engineer and a witch with me. Barah is our best pilot, I might need his skills to get out."

"And Alise?"

"If I'm trapped over there and there's anything alive on it, a hunter would be handy, don't you think?"

"I do think. Not taking a healer?"

"I'm the healer. I've spent a lot of time in the infirmary helping Alore. I can't take her with me, Chella needs her now, but I can manage if I have to."

The old man nodded his agreement. "You chose well. Do you want a warrior?"

"No, you're first man, you have to stay here too. I won't take any chances, Poppa Rath, I promise."

Deann left the bridge and headed for the fighter bay. She stopped off at the infirmary to let Michella know what was up, then continued on her way. That was the last time Michella would ever see the Deann she knew. The woman who would return to her a few weeks later would be very different; older, wiser, and a lot more savage.

The crew was waiting for her when she reached the bay. She climbed aboard the fighter and Barah took her out. Deann could see that Pally, like his father, had stocked the small ship with as many supplies and spare parts as she could carry. "Approaching derelict ship," said Barah, as they drew nearer to the monster that hung in space. "Repeat, approaching derelict ship. Warbird, acknowledge." There was nothing but static.

"The energy field around her must be interfering with the comms," mused Deann. "Is it affecting us?"

"No, we seem to be fine, Captain," replied Alise.

"Damn thing is just too blasted big," muttered Deann as she gazed out the view port. "Any sign of a docking port?"

"None so far," replied Barah. "There's some arrays up ahead, might be something there."

"Take a closer look. We still okay, Alise?"

"All good, Captain Deann."

Suddenly the small fighter powered down and lurched sideways. "Skeet," swore Barah, as he tried to regain power. The small fighter was pulled inexorably to the huge ship. A port opened and they were pulled inside. As soon as the port closed behind them their power came back up. "Dammit, we're trapped inside."

"Easy now," said Deann. "It must have been an automatic docking system. Once it had us safely inside it released us. Probably was used for bringing supplies aboard. I don't see a launch bay or anything else handy. Before we go exploring, nose her up to that port again and see if it will let us out." It didn't.

Barah started cursing again, but Nellie laid a gentle hand on his shoulder. He settled down immediately. "Well then, it looks like exploring is our only option unless you want to try shooting our way out."

"No, somehow I don't think that would work. I'd like to conserve our weapons for now. Let's go exploring. Alise, anything interesting on sensors?"

"We seem to be oriented along the long axis of the ship, Captain. "I'm picking up a lot of damage, some rubble, plenty of plant life and some animal life. For a second I thought I had a human life sign, but I can't be sure."

"Hmm, Nellie, you get anything?"

The small witch closed her eyes and let her awareness reach out. A few minutes later she opened her eyes. "There's lots of animal life, some alien that I don't understand. It's not Korim nor Fellie, and there's a number of humans. They aren't near, but they're on this ship."

"Okay, so let's go see if we can find the humans. They should have lots of information about this monster that can help us. Alise, keep an eye out for another port to the outside, too. We might get lucky." They didn't.

They flew deeper into the massive ship. "I wonder what's keeping the lights on?" mused Pally.

"I was wondering that myself," said Deann. "Sensors say anything good about air in the place?"

"There's an atmosphere and it's breathable," replied Nellie.

"You sure about that?"

"Dee, there are humans in here running around without atmo suits. We can breathe the air."

"Good to know. Thanks Nellie."

"Stop," said Alise. Barah stopped and hovered the ship high in the air.

"Talk to me, Alise."

"Captain, there's an open space ahead where we could land. There's forest close by with many animals. There are plenty of human life signs, ten close by and sixty or more farther away. There are five ships about the size of the Warbird with the humans. Also, there are about thirty alien life signs closing on the ten humans. The humans are watching us. They're unaware of the aliens approaching."

"Nellie, hail them."

"Comms are down, Captain."

"Skeet. Barah, drop us down by our cousins. We'll have to do this the hard way."

Red Novans

The small ship dropped down and landed lightly a few feet away from the group of men. They all drew their weapons. Deann hopped to the ground and gave them her best smile. "Hi there. Do you folks have any enemies on this ship?"

"Plenty and nothing but," replied the nearest man, a grim look on his face. "Spy. Get on the ground, face first, arms spread. Now."

"No wait," begged Deann, using her best frightened little girl voice, "you have to ..."

"Shut the hell up and get on the ground," replied the man, as he slapped her across the face, knocking her over backwards. Her own crew were under guard and couldn't help her. Nellie suddenly looked away to stifle a giggle. Deann had winked at her.

"Please, you have to listen," Deann said, a quiver in her voice as she reached imploringly towards the man.

"I said shut the hell up," he shouted, as he grabbed the front of her tunic to haul her to her feet. That's when his world changed forever. As he pulled her up she fairly flew into the air. Powerful thighs clamped tightly around his neck and her body twisted to the side. He was ripped off his feet, spun through the air to land heavily on his back, her blade at his throat.

Her voice was like ice when she spoke. "Drop your weapons or I'll kill him. Now!" Reluctantly the others obeyed. "Now that I have your attention, there are twenty or more alien life forms closing on us fast. Are they friend or foe?"

The man swallowed hard before he choked out an answer. It was a single word. "Foe."

Deann was off him in a heartbeat, barking orders. "Barah, Nellie, get the ship in the air. Pally, Alise, behind that pile of rubble." She spun to face her opponent. "Get your men behind that junk there." He didn't respond so she turned to the others. "Go! We'll get them in a crossfire." She grabbed the former leader by the front of his shirt. "You're with me. We'll tease them into chasing us. That'll pull them into the kill zone."

She stepped away from him, turning her back so she could face the direction of the oncoming aliens. A moment later he was beside her, his weapon in his hand. "Who in the nine hells are you, woman?"

"Deann of Nova," she replied.

His voice was strangely sad when he replied. "I truly wish you were the matriarch. Maybe then we might stand a chance of survival."

"What makes you say that?"

"Deann of Nova was the first of our clan, Red Nova. It was from her that a hundred generations sprang, fighters, warriors, defenders of all Novans, and now the last surviving Novans."

"You have a story to tell, my friend, and I do want to hear it, but first we have to deal with whatever is headed our way. There they are now."

"You can see them through that fallen bulkhead?"

"I have a special eye under this patch. It lets me see what you can't. So tell me, what am I fighting? What are their skills, attributes, weapons?"

"We call them Tangles. They're big, strong, but slow moving. Their weapons shoot out tentacles that tangle you up and burn like hellfire. Once burned you're condemned to a slow death."

"Your healers not good against burns?"

"The tangles killed our last healer two years past. Dammit, there they are. There's far too many of them. Dornal, get the men out of here."

He started to run, but Deann tripped him and he fell headlong. "Dornal, belay that. Hold your ground," she shouted. "Get on your feet, you. If you're one of my descendants then act like it."

"Dammit, woman, they're almost ..."

He got no further as Deann drew a weapon he hadn't seen and opened fire. One of the aliens fell. She shot another and they charged. Suddenly she heard the crackle of the blaster beside her as he joined the fight. "Ah, to the nine hells with it," he snarled, as he continued firing, "today is a good day as any to die."

Deann grabbed his arm and dragged him away. "Now we run." She pounded away, with him on her heels. The aliens gave chase and were drawn right into the zone where she wanted them. "Fire!" she screamed, as she turned to face the oncoming horde.

Weapons fire erupted from both sides and above. The confusion caused the enemy to mill about for a moment and by then it was too late. The small fighter ship swooped in and raked them with bullets and energy fire. The humans fired from both sides. The few who tried to escape were run down and killed by Deann and her companion.

Deann stood looking down at the body of an alien. It was large with four arms, loose floppy ears, and big eyes set far apart. "This poor thing isn't built quite right," she said. Her companion chuckled at that. "So, what did you say your name is?"

"I'm Quint, latest chieftain of the last of the Red Novans."

"Yeah, about that story. I know there's a lot more of you folks not too far from here. Tell me now, am I going to have any more trouble from you? Do I have to beat up the lot of you?"

"No, ma'am," he chuckled. "You've defeated the chieftain, didn't kill him, then you brought us a victory without losing a man. What are your orders?"

"Take us back to your people. We can exchange stories, then put our heads together and find a way off this damn derelict."

"Yes, well, we can certainly exchange stories. The rest might not be so easy."

"Have you got comms?"

"Don't work so well anymore," he replied. "I'll send a runner on ahead." He turned and called out to the youngest of the men. "Feek, head home and let the folk know we're on our way, we have company, they're friends, and they have a small fighter ship. Tell them not to fire on it." The young fellow grinned, saluted, and sped away.

They walked along a pathway through a forest of strange plants. Quint plucked a fruit from a small tree and offered it to her. Deann gave it a doubtful look, but he took a huge bite then pulled another and passed it to her. She noticed the other men doing the same, so she took a tentative bite. It was sweet and juicy. She smiled and nodded her thanks.

A small animal darted out into the path and something whizzed past Quint's ear. He turned with wide eyes to see Alise grinning. She nodded ahead and he turned to see the animal dead in the path, an arrow through its heart. "Meat for the pot," she said. He nodded and swept it up as he passed by. He pulled out the bloody arrow and passed it back.

There was a full gathering by the time they arrived. The ships stood silently guarding the open space between them. This was obviously their main camp. The alien trees were tall enough to hide the ship from an observer in the air. They were greeted by a wall of armed fighters, no old, children, or pregnant women to be seen. "Bring them all out," shouted Quint. "These folks are friends, maybe more."

"What do you mean, more?" demanded an older fellow, as he stepped forward.

"This woman claims to be Deann of Nova," replied Quint. "I'm damn near to believing her. She whipped my buttocks then took command and led us against the Tangles. We were outnumbered by two to one, yet we have the victory with no injured. It was a victory worthy of the ancestors."

The older fellow put away his weapon and stepped close to Deann. "How can this be?" he asked softly. "It can't be true, can it?"

"Why the hells not," asked Quint. "The damn thing's a time ship, isn't it?"

The older fellow nodded then looked at the others for a moment then back to Deann. Slowly he sank to one knee as did all the others. "Have you come to deliver us, Matriarch?"

"Hey now, cut this out. Get up, for pity's sake. First of all, I can't be a matriarch, I still haven't born a child. Second, we discovered this giant ship in our territory. We came to get a closer look and were pulled inside. Yes, we want back out and you're certainly welcome to come with us. Now, stand up and tell me who you are, all of you, your people."

The old fellow stood and smiled gently. "So young yet. I see it now. You still wear the Gold Nova marks, don't you? Mine are red, all our marks are red. We're Red Nova, your children, well, your descendants after about a hundred generations." He pulled aside his tunic to show her the red sunburst of Nova.

Deann nodded and showed him her tattoos. "Who and what are you?" she asked.

"I'm Eddan," he replied. "I am, or was, an historian of the Red Nova. You're my ancestress, the creator of Red Nova."

Deann shook her head slowly. "My head hurts. Nellie, help me make sense of this."

The small witch stepped close to her friend and captain. "Dee, I think I'm getting a handle on it. Quint said this is a time ship. It looks like we stumbled on a bunch of our own descendants. Our future is ancient history to these folks."

"Our future?"

"Well, one possible future. The future's not set. Every time any of us makes a decision it'll affect the future. The mere chance we've met these folks will change the timeline they came from."

"You're not helping."

"Sorry. Okay, let me try again. These folks are our offspring. They're trapped here and so are we. If we find a way off this monster we could be in their time, our time, or somewhere else completely. So, for the time being, think of them as our folk, and they need our help just as we need theirs."

"Okay, stop. Stop right there. I can work with that. I'll absorb the rest of it in pieces later. Right now we have work to do." Nellie patted her shoulder and stepped back.

Deann turned to Quint. "So, Quint, you're the one in charge here?"

"No, you are."

"What??? Look, start making sense, mister, or I'll have to beat the snot out of you again."

Quint grinned as he stepped closer. "Matriarch, our last true chieftain died years ago when he defeated the Iron Emperor. Since then there have been several chieftains, but the Tangles keep reducing our numbers and the chieftains keep getting killed. That would have been my fate today if you hadn't taken charge. Lady, I'm a good fighter, but I'm no chieftain. I don't have the head nor the knack for it. You do. You defeated me, so that makes you the chieftain."

"Now hold on here ..."

Deann was startled to hear Nellie's voice in her mind. She knew of this talent, but had never experienced it before. "Dee, wait. This is the best solution. These folks are kin, but they're broken and defeated. Look at them, Dee. They need a leader, and they need hope. You can give them that, besides, if we're ever going to get out of this mess you'll be the one to lead us out."

Deann nodded, her mind racing. No one spoke or tried to disturb her. Finally she sighed, a tear in her eye. Angrily she brushed it aside and accepted her fate. At last she spoke. "Is this truly what you want? All of you?"

As one they knelt, men, women, and children. "Hail Deann of Nova, Chieftain of Red Nova, Matriarch."

"All right, I accept this. Nellie, I need you."

Nellie stepped up beside her. "Dee?"

"Change my tats to red." Nellie's eyes widened, but Deann nodded. Nellie placed her hand on Deann's neck and sang a high sweet note. When she took her hand away Deann's tattoos were of a red sunburst. She showed them to the people nearest to her. They all began to cheer.

The people were still kneeling and Deann sighed. "Stand up, people. You kneel to your priestess only, never me. Got it?"

"Lady, we have no priestess. There hasn't been a witch among the Novans for generations."

Deann watched Quint's face as he spoke. Although he spoke to her his eyes were on Nellie. She turned to Nellie who had seen. Nellie's eyes were wide as Deann gave her the *look*. Finally she sighed and nodded. "Okay, Dee. You're probably right about this."

"Some robes might be a bit more impressive," whispered Deann.

"Fine," grumbled Nellie, as her jumpsuit suddenly morphed into black robes, flame dancing around her small figure.

"Maybe something a bit more friendly?" suggested Deann. Nellie made a face at her, then the robes lightened to red and the flames died. "Hear me, my people," said Deann, as she held Nellie's hand high. "This woman is a powerful witch, and she is now your priestess. She is Lady Nellie of Red Nova."

Nellie made another face at her then stepped forward. "People, we are Red Nova. We need no temple in this accursed ship. We'll build one when we find a better home. So, for now there'll be no need to kneel before me unless I'm wearing these robes of office." She turned slowly so all could see her then her robes morphed back into her jumpsuit. She smiled then stepped back beside Barah.

"Well, that's bloody well done it," he muttered. "Better make my tats red, too." She nodded them placed her hand on his shoulder. He felt a slight sting then it was done. Pally touched her shoulder lightly. When she turned to him he nodded. She changed his tattoos as well.

As Alise smiled shyly at her, she nodded then gave the Korim girl red Tattoos to match Pally's.

Deann smiled her thanks then turned back to her new people. "Red Nova's chieftain is hungry. Our hunter has brought meat, will no one help her cook it?"

"Get a fire up," bellowed Quint. "Bring out the spit."

Alise sidled closer to Deann. "Captain, that one small animal won't feed all these people."

"Then you'd better get busy," grinned Deann. "Quint, who's your best hunter?"

"That would be Dornal. Dor, over here." The young man trotted up, gave Deann his most winning smile, then quirked an eyebrow.

"This woman is Alise, our hunter," said Deann. "Show her the trails, bring us more meat."

"Yes, ma'am." He winked at her then led Alise into the forest.

Deann turned to Quint. "What kind of shape are your ships in?"

"All five can fly, but we barely have enough people left to properly man three. They're low on fuel and weapons, most of the supplies are gone, only two have shields. In truth, I wouldn't want to try a prolonged journey in one."

"What about the inertial dampeners?"

He just snorted. "We haven't had those for a couple of generations now. The last of the inertia ships was decommissioned in my great grandsire's time."

"Why?"

"They couldn't make them, Dee," said Pally. "You need a strong witch to make the right chips, remember?"

"Right. Quint, give Pally a tour of the ships. He's a fine engineer and the man who invented the inertial dampeners. Pally, see what you can do to make three good ships out of the five."

"On it, boss." He followed Quint into one of the ships and Deann sank down to put her back to a tree.

"Nellie, what the hell have I gotten myself into this time?" she asked, as Nellie sat beside her.

"You? You mean what have you gotten all of us into?"

"Aw, I'd just be lonely without you."

"Fool," laughed Nellie as she swatted Deann's shoulder. "You gave in pretty easy, Dee."

"It was you, girl. You made me look at them. I saw Jip's sad face times fifty looking back at me. You're right, they're beaten, broken, and they desperately need hope. We need them to help us get off this damn ship. It did seem like the only way. I guess the rest of you guys could see that, too."

"Yeah, we could."

"So you all threw in with me."

"Dee, we're in a hard spot, here. If we're going to get out alive, it'll be because you were leading us. As much as I love and admire Chella, I'd rather see you in the captain's chair when it all goes nasty. You're a natural leader, you've got good instincts, and you're lucky."

"Lucky? You call this lucky?"

"Sure. This morning you were just the back up captain on the Warbird. Now you're chieftain of a bigger clan than Chella's father."

"Yeah, lucky me. Nellie ..."

"I'm beside you all the way in this, Dee. We all are. You're the captain. You're the chieftain. Take command and get this done."

"Get it done," mused Deann. "I guess the first step is to keep everybody alive. Next will be to get those ships in the air and find a way out."

"Ah-huh. Dee, have you noticed anything?"

"Yeah I have, Nellie, and it's bothering me."

"The big ship's not completely dead."

"Yep, that would be it. Life support is still running. Who knows what else could still be functional."

A Bit of History

Deann was lost in thought for a while and Nellie didn't disturb her. Finally she looked up. "You and Barah take the ship up and make sure we don't have any extra guests coming for dinner."

Nellie grinned as she rose. "Aye, Captain," she said, in that sexy purr she used on all the Warbird's comm announcements. It brought a laugh of delight from Deann.

As Nellie and Barah headed to the small ship, Deann caught Eddan's eye and beckoned him over. He came and sat beside her. "All right, Eddan, I think I'm ready for a bit more history. Give it to me slowly and in proper order."

He chuckled then began. "Yes, Chieftain. I can understand that this is both confusing and overwhelming. Where do you want to start?"

"Where Nova Clan split into two parts. Work from there."

He nodded. "It began with the capture and rape of the great chieftain's daughter, companion to Deann of Nova, and the child to come from that rape. At that time Deann, you, learned she could command. Indeed she was born to lead. The child was a wedge between the lovers and Deann eventually left the Novans rather than be near the child.

"Several of the Novans went with her. They fought a pitched battle against pirates, most were killed on both sides. Deann took those who were left, both Novan and pirate, to a place where they could survive. There she bore her first child. As things deteriorated and the Novans came under great pressure Deann returned to fight beside them. The Black Witch accepted them as a separate clan of her people and gave them the red marks.

"Michella's son grew up and became the first of the Blue Novans."

"Blue Novans? There's blue now?"

"No longer. The blues were artists, singers, dancers, sculptors, and the like, not fighters."

"Okay, Eddan, slow down now. You're saying the kid's not a problem child?"

"You mean the first blue? No, he was a delight to everyone, according to the histories."

"All right. So, I left Nova Clan and started my own? I have some Novans with me?"

"They are here with you now, Matriarch, the engineer, the hunter, the pilot and the witch."

"Nellie says the future's not set. If we make different decisions we can change the future."

"So, that's why you want to know what happened?"

"Eddan, I'm still trying to believe all this. Oh relax, I'm getting there. You said the Novans prospered for generations, yes?"

"Yes. At first it was difficult as Sega Clan pushed them hard, but they prospered and grew."

"Wait, Sega Clan? How did they get involved?"

"It was the time of the old king, Borad of Arcalia. Sega Clan had him assassinated then caused an uprising. They walked in and took over. Nova Clan lost her greatest ally and supply channels."

"I see. Okay, we'll keep that bit for later in case we get back to my time. Now tell me how we ended up here in this ghost ship."

"That began with the return of the Iron Emperor. The great chieftain had defeated him and sent him across the universe in exile."

"Yeah, I was there for that part of it."

"Yes, well, he managed to find and commandeer this time ship, conquered and enslaved vast armies of the Tangle people and others. He wanted to come back to face his old enemy again, but he missed the timing. He arrived in our time. By then the Novans numbered in the tens of thousands. He also missed his mark and arrived in the middle of the Sector Nine armada. He defeated them easily then turned his attention to the Novans. In the first strike he obliterated the Golds and the Blues, as well as most of the Reds.

"During that final battle, Rogan, our chieftain, led five war ships through a port and into this ship. We fought our way inside where we got slaughtered by the emperor himself. We fled deep into the ship. He came after us and Rogan challenged him to single combat. It was a desperate ploy, but it worked. Rogan managed to maneuver him close to an air lock. We blew the lock open with missiles and both combatants were sucked out into space before the automatic seals closed the lock. Both men are now floating around out there somewhere or somewhen."

"They're not men, Eddan. At least the emperor wasn't. He's a robot, can't be destroyed, immortal. The chieftain managed to render him helpless, but no more. If some idiot salvages him and brings him into a warm environment ..." Eddan just gazed at her with wide eyes. "Anyway, that's not our problem right now. What happened after you blew him out the airlock?"

Eddan sighed and resumed his tale. "By this time we were cut off from the bridge. Pursued and attacked from all sides, we fought back as best we could, eventually securing this small encampment here in the far reaches of the ship. Most of our fuel is gone, our weapons depleted, and we're vastly outnumbered. We can't get out, and they just keep coming."

"How long have you folk been trapped here?"

"Nearly twenty years."

"When was the last time any of those ships flew?"

"About ten years, give or take."

She thought for a minute then a look of deep concern crossed her face. "Eddan, how many of your people could actually fly a ship?"

"Our people, Matriarch," he said gently.

"Yes, sorry. I need a bit more adjustment time. Our people. I'm not seeing a lot of older folk. And I'm betting the younger ones have never worked a live ship."

"You're everything the histories say you were," he smiled. "Actually, I'm beginning to think they didn't do you justice. You're right. Since our current survival depends more on hunting and avoiding the enemy, we've focused on keeping the ships on the ground, ready for that one last race to freedom should the happy chance come our way. The ships are primarily automated, and two men could fly one. They couldn't fight, but they could run."

"Understood. However, it's not good enough. As soon as Pally declares a ship ready we begin training flight crews. Every man, woman, and child needs to know, and be comfortable with, every station on those ships."

She got no further as a great shout went up. Dornal entered the camp staggering under the weight of a dead beast of immense proportions. Alise walked along beside him, a huge grin on her face and a brace of smaller animals lashed together and slung across her back. A cheer went up and several people leaped to help dress out and prepare the meat.

Deann smiled and rose to her feet. She waved her arm overhead and the small ship dropped lightly to the ground. The feast was about to get underway.

Everyone ate their fill for the first time in a long time. Once they were all settled back, resting, a loud round of laughter broke out. A loud protest was followed by another round of laughter. As it settled down Quint called out to Deann. "Chieftain." She looked up and, a wide grin on his face, he continued. "Chieftain, these hardened warriors don't believe I was trying when we fought. They think I was besotted by a beautiful young woman." That brought on more laughter.

"This could be a problem," muttered Pally.

"The hell it will," replied Deann, as she rose to her feet. As she approached the men the laughter subsided swiftly. Deann wasn't smiling. "Which of you think it wasn't real?" No one answered, nor would they meet her eyes. She stepped to the side where there was open ground. "Quint, choose four men, the best you've got."

Everyone was quiet now. What had started in fun wasn't anymore. No one wanted to upset the new chieftain, but it was too late for that. Quint pointed to four men and, reluctantly they stepped out. "Chieftain, we were just having a bit of fun with old Quint. We didn't mean ..."

"Defend yourselves."

"What???"

"Defend yourselves. Use any weapons you want." They were still looking stunned when she moved. Deann took two running strides towards the men then dived to the ground in a forward roll. She came out of the roll and drove her fist into the first man's testicles. Spinning on her back she lashed out, her boot smashing into another man's hamstring. As he fell she climbed his body and swung herself high over his head to land easily on the ground behind him.

She dove for the next man's knees, but he grabbed her around the waist and lifted her high into the air. Deann shifted her attack on the fly, wrapping her legs around the man's neck and throwing her upper body past his head, taking him off balance. He was whipped through the air to land face down, driving the air from his lungs.

She ducked and rolled away as the last man made a grab for her. She turned and rolled back against him, throwing him slightly off balance. He grabbed for her and she swung herself into the air, locking her legs around his neck and twisting sharply. Like Quint before him, he was whipped through the air to land heavily on his back with a blade at his throat.

Deann rolled away and came to her feet facing the amazed and stunned audience. There were grunts and groans behind her, but she ignored them. "This is unacceptable," she said loudly. "I could probably take the lot of you all myself. The gods help you if the rest of my crew gets involved.

"You call yourselves Red Nova, the fighting clan. Well then, that's exactly who we'll be. Training starts tomorrow, first day shift. Every man, woman, and child will train. When Red Nova leaves this accursed time ship, we will leave as the most powerful and deadly fighting force this universe has ever seen. We have no idea what we'll face when we leave here, but I promise you, we'll be ready for it." She turned and walked away.

"What do you think, Pally?" she asked, as she sank to the ground beside him once again. "Too much?"

"Impressive and then some," he grinned in reply, "but, no, not too much. I think they've got the idea now."

Alise leaned closer. "Captain Deann, you must return to them now. If you don't they will hate and fear you. If you go to them as one of them they will worship you. I have seen Krak'sul do this before."

Deann thought for a moment then patted Alise on the shoulder as she rose. She headed back to the men, stopping to pick up a strip of meat on the way by. She walked in among them and sat beside Dornal. She gave him a friendly nudge with her shoulder. "Hey Dor, that guy flips easier than Quint."

Dornal chuckled then spoke. "Chieftain, can you teach me that move. I wouldn't mind flipping old Quint once or twice." Quint responded with a bellowing laugh.

"You guys okay?" asked Deann. "I tried not to injure anybody."

"Not to injure?" asked the man, who'd been flipped onto his back. "You damn near broke my neck."

"Aw come on, I flipped Quint then made him fight a battle. Are you saying you couldn't do that?"

"I'm saying I'm going to kill that lying historian for telling us you were just a great warrior. I think he held a bit of information back."

Eddan laughed. "Not my fault. The histories weren't complete on the Matriarch's fighting skills."

"No skeet," grumbled another. That brought another round of laughter.

Dornal was enjoying being so close to the new super chieftain, especially since she was about his age. Deann felt his attraction to her, but didn't discourage it. She needed all these people on side and that couldn't hurt. "So tell me, chieftain, where did you learn to fight like that?"

"Do the histories ever speak of Rathbone of Urn?"

"Not that I'm aware of," replied Eddan.

"Hmm. Well, back in my time there was an assassin named Rathbone of Urn. He was quite old when I met him. Poppa Rath was the most feared man in the galaxy. The mention of his name could send people scrambling in terror. If Rathbone of Urn was after you, you were already dead. He taught me to fight, and to kill. He taught me how to control the emotions of battle, or assassination, how to be greater than I was."

"An assassin, by his very nature, would want to be paid," said Eddan. "What was his price?"

"He taught me so all the skills he had learned over his long life wouldn't pass into oblivion once he died. I swore to pass the knowledge on in turn so that what he'd learned would never die. Starting tomorrow morning, I begin to keep that promise.

"You see my engineer over there? That's Palentine, great grandson of the assassin. Old Rath is a small man, like Dor here, just a little fella."

"Hey now," said Dornal, laughing and blushing at the same time.

"Pally is built like his father, Rathbone the younger. Young Rath is a terrifying sight to behold when he comes at you. He has a lot of fighting skills, and he enjoys getting into the rough stuff. He passed that training and skill on to his son. Pally will be working with you bigger fellas. His fighting style will suit you better. I'll work with the smaller men, the women, and kids."

Deann noticed the look on Dornal's face and grinned. "Hey there, don't get all sulky on me. When I'm finished with you all these big guys will wet themselves when you come at them." That brought another round of laughter.

"I think there's something else you men might want to know about Captain Deann," said Pally, as he joined them.

"What's that?" asked Dornal.

"Dee's far more than a fighter. Yes, she killed a giant in single combat and more, but that's not why we follow her. We follow her because she's sharp, she can make decisions, quality decisions, in an emergency, and she's lucky."

"No such thing as luck," said Deann.

"The gospel according to my great grandfather," chuckled Pally. "She's right. Luck favors the prepared, and Deann is always prepared. Dee might not know what's coming at us, but she's always ready for anything. Quint, you saw that earlier. You and Dee were standing side by side with dozens of enemies running at you. I saw her speak. What did she say?"

Quint grinned and nodded his head. "She wanted to know what we were facing, what they were, how they fought, what weapons they had ..."

"See what I mean. She faced an enemy, greater in numbers, attributes unknown, but she didn't panic. The captain's mind is always working, thinking, looking for the weakness to exploit. In other words, my great grandsire's training at work.

"My father often said that it is a better life to follow a leader who has a purpose than to run free on your own. That's why he follows the man he does. That's why I follow Deann."

"As will we all, and gladly," said Quint. "Most of these people have never known any other life but this ship. For the first time in a lot of years I'm suddenly hopeful we might eventually escape this death trap. I have no idea where or when we'll end up, but I'd rather take my chances out there. Deann, we've all accepted you as our chieftain. We're sincere in that and won't hold back."

"I know," she replied, an easy smile on her lips. "I know. We'll start tomorrow. I don't have stars in my eyes or anything. I know it's going to take some time to get this done, but we will get it done."

"So, got a plan, Dee?" asked Pally.

"Working on it. First thing we have to do is to get one of the big ships ready then train everybody on how to fly it."

"You'll be wanting the inertial dampeners on it, right?"

"Right."

"It's going to take a while. I'll need Nellie and Barah."

"I know, take some of the new folks too, they need to learn how this is done, but don't take too long. While you're working on that I want to map out the inside of this monster. The damn thing is still running and that's a good thing right now, but when we leave we leave it dead." The gathered men and women nodded their approval.

The lights didn't dim or brighten, so they went by ship's time. Guards were set out and everybody else headed for the bunks on the ships. The largest ship was the flagship. Quint cleared out the chieftain's quarters for Deann. The best of the rest went to her small crew. Next morning Deann and Pally were standing in the open space between the ships when the klaxons sounded the first shift.

"Move it, people," bellowed Pally's deep bass voice. "Your chieftain is all alone in the training area and she's not happy."

People came pouring out of the ships. Deann stood with her arms folded while Pally worked. He swiftly separated the larger men into one group and the smaller men, able women, and older boys into another. Nellie appeared and took the pregnant women, small children, and three elders aside to eat.

There was a bit of grumbling in the ranks. "How come they get to eat before exercise?" Deann heard and fought to suppress a grin.

"All right people, listen to me. As warriors, our duty is to protect and nourish our young and elders. They eat first. We're the strong. Our task is to provide for them then make certain they're safe to enjoy it. We do this so when we're old and gray they'll do the same for us." That brought a round of chuckles. "All right, Pally's group, step over and give us a bit of room. My group, step this way."

The first day of training was mostly stretching then some strength moves. When they finished Deann addressed them again. "Well done, family. Today was the first step in a long journey. We'll make that journey one step at a time. Barah, you and Alise go up for a look-see. Dornal, bring in the night guards, then get some food. I'll work their training myself."

An hour later the men who'd had the last watch were finished the training and settling down to eat. The fighter was on the ground, her crew was fed, then Deann went to eat. Quint and Eddan came to sit beside her. "The chieftain eats last?" asked Eddan.

"It's a tough job," replied Deann. "Yes, the elders, pregnant women, children eat first, then the warriors, and last the chieftain. As long as we're not sure of our supplies this is the way it has to be. Once Alise gets the larder full of meat we can ease up on that rule a bit."

"We'll need to gather veg too," said Quint, "and fruit."

"That hard to do?"

"Not if you can avoid the predators and the Tangles."

Deann chewed thoughtfully for a moment. "Alise brought home a bunch of meat last night. Any left?"

"Lots," replied Eddan.

"Any veg in stores?"

"Enough for three days maybe."

She nodded slowly. "All right, every third day we'll all break into two groups. One to hunt and one to harvest. We do this until we have our supplies topped up. On the other days we work on getting the ships ready to fly and the people ready to fly them."

"Do you have a plan to get the ships out into open space again?" asked Quint.

"Not yet. First I need information. We need to map this monster, find the main bridge and figure out how to work it."

"You want to take control of the intergalactic ship?"

"No, I want to escape and destroy it. We need the main bridge so we can shut off the automatics and open an airlock big enough to let us escape."

"That would mean someone has to stay behind to operate the locks. That's a job for me."

"In a hurry to meet your maker, Quint?" asked Deann.

"Not really. Have you got a better idea?"

"I was thinking Pally might be able to rig up a remote to operate the lock and then set off the self-destruct."

Quint grinned. "I do like that plan better."

"Okay men, let's get down to business. Quint, send your five best engineers to help Pally with the ships. He'll put them to work where he has the most need. Find Barah and send him to me, he'll be with Pally." He nodded and started to rise, but she caught his arm. "Once the engineers are on their way, bring me your three best hunters. After that, you and I'll begin inspecting the weapons." Quint grinned and rose to do her bidding.

Deann turned to Eddan. "Now, sir, about the histories, have you taught the children?"

"None seemed interested."

"They don't have a choice. Set up a school and start teaching them. Half hour of class then a half hour of play incorporating the lesson then another half hour of class. They need to be fully literate and to know their history. As they age we'll move on to other studies like engineering, weapons manufacture, ship building, etc. You have access to this knowledge, do you not?"

"Some of it, Chieftain, but ..."

Deann smiled and patted his arm. "Start with what you have. We'll worry about the rest when we get to it. Eddan, in the evenings teach any of the adults who want to learn."

"Yes, ma'am. I'll get started right now. Here come your hunters."

Alise trotted up, three of the Red Novans close behind her. Dornal was among them. He gave her a bright smile and a wink. Deann stood and stretched. "Dor, tell me I'm not going to have to whip your butt to make you understand I'm bonded to another."

"I'm aware, Chieftain, but it'll be a long time before we can escape the time ship and when we do we may not be in your time."

Deann just looked back at him sadly and he instantly regretted his words. Before he could stammer an apology Barah came trotting up. "You wanted me, Dee?"

"How's our fighter for fuel?"

"Topped up and we brought spare fuel rods, why?"

"I want this ship mapped. Alise, you know how to do this?"

"You want to know where there is food, water, forest, open spaces, enemies, encampments, air locks, entry and exit ports, control areas ..."

"That's it exactly," replied Deann, giving the Korim girl a smile of approval. "You can't just keep it in your memory, you have to log it so I can study it too. I'm sending you because you'll know what to look for. These men are your assistants. They'll guide you and obey your commands."

"Of course." Alise beamed her pleasure at Deann's praise.

"Barah, your job is to pilot the ship under duress, but make Dor fly her otherwise. Teach him well. I've just decided he'll fly one of the big ships out of here. Keep him busy. Keep him out of trouble."

"So I'm babysitting."

"You're the best pilot Nova Crew Two ever had and you know it. Now you teach others. Barah, we need pilots."

"You're right, Dee. Sorry."

"Go on now. Alise is in command, but you can train pilots while she maps out the ship. Once Dor is ready you can go back to helping in engineering."

Deann walked away and Alise leaped aboard the small ship. "Let's get started." The others followed her aboard and Barah took the controls. The small ship leaped into the air. "There's no point going back where we've already been. Align us on the long axis of the time ship." the fighter turned slightly.

Alise looked all around, consulted her sensors, then tapped some information into the tablet in her hand. She reached out to touch the man closest to her. "You are Pierce?"

"Yes."

"You know well, the area close to the compound."

"Yes."

"Then we have no need to explore it. What is that way?"

"Forest for a ways, but then mostly open spaces, abandoned storage for several levels."

Alise nodded. "Pilot, turn one quarter left then proceed one kilometer." The ship turned clumsily, Dornal at the controls.

Dor sat quietly at the controls, trying to memorize what Barah had told him. He was nervous and it showed. Finally Barah took pity on him. While Alise inspected eighty-three levels through a central shaft, and Dor slowly became more at ease with the controls, Barah leaned across his shoulder and spoke softly. "Dor, if you think Captain Deann is hell on wheels, you should see her partner, Mamma Chella. If you ever meet her, don't make her angry."

Dornal swallowed hard and nodded, keeping his eyes on the controls. Barah sighed and went on. "Look, I know we could be years escaping this trap. Dee knows it too. Give her time, stay friendly, but don't push. If she wants you, she'll come to you in her own time."

"And if I push?"

"She'll probably kill you. Dee's all soft and girlish most of the time, but she goes cold and deadly when annoyed or in battle. You only got a sample of that yesterday. I've seen her at all out war."

"Right, friendly and respectful. Look, I don't want to ..."

"I know. Deann is gorgeous, but deadly. If you want to play that game, you should know what you're getting into."

"Yeah. Thanks. I think."

Barah laughed and slapped his shoulder. He sat back and took the weapons control. "I'll take guns, you've got pilot." Dornal's eyes widened and he swallowed hard again.

Finding of a Healer

Deann spent her day with the women, helping with the more domestic chores, playing with the children, and trying to remember everyone's name. As she'd hoped they soon began to relax around her. She helped prepare the evening meal then went to greet Alise and her crew of hunters as the fighter landed. "Report."

"We managed to map a small section, Chieftain," replied Alise. "The problem is, we're not working like a hunting party, we're trying to map a hollow planet. We've recorded over eighty levels, all accessible through a central shaft. However, we found nothing of value and encountered no threats."

"Well done, Alise. Get some food now and find your mate. Barah, how did Dor do on the controls?"

"Not too bad, Captain," replied Barah. "He might just make a decent pilot with a few years of practice." He chuckled and gave Dor a friendly poke in the ribs.

Deann saw the look Dor gave her before he turned away. "Maybe I'll see for myself. Dor, mount up, you're at the controls." His eyes opened wide, but he followed her into the small fighter. Deann shut the door then grabbed a pole. "Take her up, I want to have a look, make sure we're alone."

"We checked before we set her down," he said, as he took the ship up. It was smoother than she'd expected. "Alise wanted to make sure we were alone before we came down."

"I know," said Deann, as she reached past his shoulder and flipped a few switches. "I've shut off all comms and recorders. We're alone and can speak freely."

"Chieftain ..."

"Deann, or Dee, Captain Deann. I need to get used to Chieftain. Listen Dor, I'm not very good at expressing my feelings, and I'm terrible at social interactions. I'm more comfortable in a battle."

"I had noticed that."

She chuckled and poked him in the ribs. "Listen to me now. I'm bonded to another, but I'm quite aware I may never see her again. I'm also aware of your attraction to me. Dor, give me some time to sort myself out."

For the first time he looked her in the eye. He realized he was looking at the woman, not the warrior. "Forgive me if I offended you, Deann. Yes, I'm attracted to you like no one before. I can be the soul of patience. Just tell me there's a chance, no matter how small. If not ..."

"There is," she replied, squeezing his arm gently. "There is, Dor. By the time we manage to leave here Chella will have born her first child."

"The child of rape. The first of the Blue Novans."

"Yes. A child I wanted her to abort, but she wouldn't. A great distance slowly came between us, but at the last she managed to make me understand why she was determined to bear the child. What I've learned from Eddan tells me she was right all along. Dor, we reconciled, but only for a few moments before I came here. I need time to heal my heart fully. Will you grant me that?"

"Whatever you need. Ch ... I mean Deann."

"Under the circumstances I think Dee will be just fine."

"How about Dee when we're alone and Chieftain when we're not. I don't want to ruin your reputation."

He was grinning and she poked him in the ribs again. Before she could speak the sensors beeped. Deann was at the console in a heartbeat. "Skeet, get us on the ground."

He obeyed instantly and the ship dropped like a stone. It was a hard landing, but no damage done. "Battle stations, Battle stations," shouted Deann, as she leaped from the craft and raced towards the gathered folk. "Barah, Nellie, get that fighter in the air. Dor, Pally, Alise, Quint, you're with me. Battle stations people, Tangles incoming."

"Dor, lead us to where we fought them before." He sprinted away with them close behind. The rest of the fighters silently following.

"How did they find us?" wondered Quint as he puffed along beside her.

"They didn't," she replied. "I'm betting they're looking for their own people who didn't come back." They reached the place first and Deann set her people out as before. There were still plenty of dead bodies in the kill zone. She smiled a cold deadly smile. That would draw them in faster. The fighters in place on both sides of the open area, she took up her station in plain view of the enemy. Quint stood at her side and Dor appeared at the other.

"Get back with the others, Dor," she said gently.

"My place is beside my chieftain," he replied. She looked in his eyes for a moment then nodded.

Quint had watched the interplay between them. "On her right then," he said, as he stepped to Deann's left. Dor moved over.

Suddenly Deann spotted Alise leaping down from a pile of rubble and racing towards her. "Captain Deann, they have a prisoner with them. A female of the like I have not seen before. They use her harshly."

"Spread the word," replied Deann. "Keep that female alive. We want her."

"Chieftain?" asked Quint, as Alise raced away.

"If we can communicate with her, we can gain information about the enemy."

"The enemy of my enemy is my friend?"

"Something like that. Here's what we do. The others will cut them apart with the crossfire. We'll try to get in close and steal the captive."

Dor grinned. "We get the fun jobs."

"All right," said Deann. "Let's get their attention." She whipped up her blaster and fired. The enemy was still out of range of the small blaster, but the flash of light caught their eye. There were more than thirty of them. Deann sent another blast in their direction to make sure they had marked her and were moving in the proper direction. As they surged towards her she backed away slowly, firing as she went. Dor and Quint were close beside her.

The enemy swarmed towards them, but once again stopped in confusion when they got hit with the crossfire. They were slow to respond but respond they did. Their numbers had been cut, but there were still a dozen or more and they attacked with gusto once they realized what was happening. This was an enemy Red Nova knew well. The warriors fired then rolled away, ducking and dodging to avoid the lashing stingers.

Barah dove at them with the fighter ship, but Nellie called him off at the last second. "No, they have a captive. Dee wants her alive."

"Skeet. Okay, we'll make another pass. You're on guns this time. You'll know who to shoot and who not to shoot." Nellie grinned at him. Barah didn't give up the weapons easily. They swept in again and Nellie opened fire as the fighter suddenly banked then sped away.

Deann whooped with joy. Nellie had cleared the enemy away from the captive. Deann raced to the fallen woman who was trying to hide in the rubble. The girl slowly began to realize these people were defending her. She sighed and cowered lower. One slave master was like another. She didn't expect any better treatment from these aliens than she'd gotten from the others.

The battle had been short and brutal. Once again, under Deann's command, Red Nova had succeeded without a loss. Only one man was wounded. Dor was down with a bad burn on his arm.

The fight was over when Deann noticed him on his knees nursing the injury. "Well, skeeter," he sighed, a quiver in his voice. "Looks like my time's up. It was an honor to fight beside you, Chieftain."

"Bugger that," said Deann. "Get a healer over here, now."

"We don't have a healer, Chieftain," Quint replied, his voice gentle.

Deann grabbed her comms on her shoulder. "Barah, get that ship down here now." They heard nothing but static, but got the idea. The ship dropped like a stone yet landed lightly beside her. "Nellie, can you do anything with this?" she asked as Nellie appeared at her side.

"I'll try, Dee, but Ellie's the healer, not me." Nellie closed her eyes and focused her will. She sang a high note and the burn subsided, but as soon as she stopped it flared up again. Nellie tried again, but with the same result.

At this point the captive they were trying to protect crawled from her hiding place and started to run. Dor's groan of agony stopped her in her tracks. She sighed and turned back. Gently, she pushed her way through the gathered people to the wounded man. Some reached for her but Deann waved them off. The woman knelt beside Dor and took his wounded arm in her delicate fingers, lightly tracing the track of the burn and humming a high note. Dor sighed and relaxed completely. She touched his forehead and he closed his eyes. "He's sleeping," said Nellie. "She's using a healing magic I've never seen before."

The woman traced the burn again, this time singing a soft sweet note. She waved her fingers to indicate Nellie should join her. As Nellie sang the woman lifted her voice to the harmony and the burn disappeared. At that point the woman fainted. "Bring them," said Deann, as she rose to her feet. "Barah, gently now, we have wounded."

Barah and Nellie reentered the ship as Pally scooped Dor into his arms. Alise picked up the healer and carried her easily. Together they entered the small fighter while Deann led the troops back to the compound. The fighter was already there, waiting for them. As they approached the healer was awake. She cringed back against Alise, finding comfort and hopefully protection with the powerfully build Korim woman.

"Captain Deann?" asked Alise. Deann nodded. Alise seized the slave collar around the woman's neck and pulled it apart, tossing it aside. Wide eyed, she put her hand to her throat, delicately exploring her neck without the collar. "She looks half starved. Shall I feed her?"

Deann grinned as she nodded. Alise led the woman to the food where, once she understood she was allowed to eat, she tucked in with a will.

Nellie gently floated Dornal out of the small ship. The others looked on, amazed as the witch floated him over to a soft bed of moss beneath a tree. She set him down then patted Deann's arm before joining the others at the food table. There was a celebration in the compound, but Deann let it flow around her. Nellie brought her food. "The healer says he'll sleep for a while yet, but will be fine when he wakes up."

"She spoke? She can speak our language?"

"Nope."

"You could speak hers?"

"Nope."

"Nellie ..."

"This way." Nellie grinned as she tapped her forehead. She patted Deann's shoulder then returned to the celebration.

A while later Alise brought the healer to Deann. The woman, little more than a girl, knelt to inspect Dor's wound. She closed her eyes for a moment, gently moving her hand above his body, searching for more problems, but smiled brightly when she found none.

Deann studied the small woman. She was short, slight of build, with almost childlike features. Her eyes were huge, her skin pale and freckled, and her ears were closely fitted to her skull, but tall and upswept. She had long graceful fingers and her voice was sweet and musical. She was chatting to the sleeping man now. Deann had no idea what she was saying.

The woman looked up at her and smiled tentatively, hopefully. Deann returned the smile and the woman began to chatter away. Deann laughed with delight, but held up a hand to stop her. "Deann," she said as she pointed to her own chest. She then pointed to the woman with a upraised eyebrow. She got the idea.

"Leen," she said softly. She pointed at Deann. "Deann." And then to herself. "Leen."

Deann smiled and nodded. "Deann, Leen, Dor." She pointed to the sleeping man. "Alise." She pointed past the woman's shoulder. Leen smiled with delight and began pointing. "Deann, Dor, Leen, Alise." Within the hour she'd learned the name of every Novan in the clan and, as Deann would come to learn, Leen never forgot anything, ever.

Within a week the strange healer was able to manage the language. Alise brought her to Deann one morning after exercises. "Leen wants to talk to you, Captain Deann."

Deann smiled and sank to the ground in a cross-legged position. She patted the ground and Leen sat facing her. Alise joined them. "So, what's on your mind, Leen?" asked Deann.

The elfin woman thought for a moment before she spoke. Finally she met Deann's gaze. "Alise tell Leen of Novan's finding Alise people. Novans like Alise people. Alise people like Novans. Novans adopt Alise people. Alise find Pally. Alise happy Novan."

Deann smiled and nodded so Leen went on. "Novans find Leen, take off pain collar, feed, share. Leen Like Novans. Leen be Novan?"

"You want to be adopted into the clan?"

"Yes, yes, adopt to clan. Leen be Novan."

"Leen, do you understand we are a warrior people?"

The woman looked thoughtful for a moment, absorbing the question, making sure she understood. Suddenly she brightened. "Yes, yes, warrior Novans. Much fighting. Plenty work for good healer. Leen best healer there is. Leen be Novan healer?"

"I like that idea," smiled Deann, as she rose to her feet. "Come." She strode into the middle of the compound then shouted. "Gather round, Red Nova. Gather round." In moments the entire clan was in the compound.

"What's up?" asked Barah.

"There's a new member of the crew," whispered Nellie. She turned and winked at Deann.

"Good people, hear me, we have a clan request. Alise." Alise seized Leen by the waist and tossed her into the air. With a squawk Leen windmilled her arms until she found solid footing on Alise's broad shoulders. Once she steadied, Deann went on. "This woman is known to you. She is Leen. She has asked to be adopted into Red Nova. What say you? Dor?"

"Keep her, Chieftain. We need a healer." He winked at Leen as he spoke.

"Quint? Eddan?"

"Keep her, Chieftain," they replied, smiling.

"Are there any objections?" There were none. "Welcome then, Leen of Red Nova, clan healer."

With a squeal of delight Leen hopped off Alise's shoulder to land in front of Deann. She scrunched her eyes closed and clenched her tiny fists for a moment. Deann was amazed to see the marks appear on Leen's bare shoulder. She had a new red sunburst. Leen opened her eyes and grinned with delight. A rousing cheer went up from the clan then they came to congratulate her one by one and she called each by their name. Deann just smiled and shook her head in amazement.

Hard Decisions

Deann had been brooding for days. She was working out, twisting, turning, leaping, and rolling so fast it was hard to follow. Blades leaped to her hands, then flew to their targets, striking with deadly accuracy. Several of the people stood by, waiting silently for her to finish. Nellie stood with them, her jumpsuit had morphed into robes.

Breathing deeply, Deann stopped, did a few stretches that astounded the onlookers then turned to them. Seeing Nellie's robes she dropped to one knee. Nellie strode up to her and raised her up. Deann turned and walked to her favorite spot beneath the tree at the edge of the compound. She sank to the ground and rested her back against the bole. She patted the ground beside her and Nellie joined her.

"What's up, Nellie? Am I scaring everybody?"

"That and then some. Dee, it's been over a year now."

"We're making progress, it's painfully slow, but it is progress."

"I know, but even if we escape tomorrow ..."

"It'll be years, Nellie, we both know that, and the gods alone know where we'll be when we do get out."

"And that brings me to the point."

"I'm the leader and my people are concerned that I'm going crazy. The way I've been throwing knives around they're starting to worry about the kids."

"Dee ..."

Deann sighed deeply. "There's no other way for it. I'm the chieftain, I won't be allowed to mourn or wallow in self pity."

"Dee, you're the matriarch. That means that, at some point, you have to bear at least one child."

"And knowing how long we could be stuck here, it's highly unlikely it will be Michella's child." She sighed again and looked away. "Dammit, it's just not fair."

"What would Poppa Rath say?"

"He'd say life's not fair, get that through your head. Life is what you make it. Stop whining and get on with it. Deal with whatever is in front of you."

"So?"

"All right, Nellie. Tell Leen to gather everybody in the compound, call in the guards, and bring Barah down to the ground. You're right. I've got to stop mourning and move on. I have a clan to think about now."

Nellie reached over and placed her hand over Deann's heart. She sent a wave of warm loving energy to her, and Deann smiled for the first time in days. Nellie then set about calling in the clan. When everyone was gathered Deann approached and knelt before Nellie. "Priestess of Red Nova, I come to beg a favor."

"What would you have of me, Chieftain?"

"Priestess, I'm bonded to another who is far away in time and space. I believe I may never see her again and would release her to find another companion."

"Then I declare the bond dissolved. Do you wish to claim another bond?" Before Deann could say anything she heard Nellie's voice in her mind. "Do it, Dee. Do it for him, for the clan, and do it for yourself. You need a companion, too."

Deann nodded. "I do."

"Then rise, Matriarch. Call forth your chosen one." Deann gave her a look and Nellie fought to suppress a giggle.

"Dor, are you near?" asked Deann, as she rose to her feet.

"Beside you," he replied. "On your right."

"Want to swear the bond with me?"

"You know I do; I always have."

Nellie stepped closer. "Dornal of Red Nova, do you swear this bond of companionship of your own free will?"

"I do so swear."

"Deann, Chieftain of Red Nova, do you swear this bond of companionship of your own free will?"

"I do so swear."

"Then I declare it so. You are bonded companions. You may now seal the bond with a kiss."

Deann stepped into his arms and he smiled. "Just don't flip me on my buttocks," he whispered as he pulled her closer. She burst out laughing then grabbed his shirt front and pulled him into a kiss. He folded her in his arms and held her gently. When their lips parted she smiled up at him then took his hand and led him away to the hoots and good-natured catcalls of the clan.

The celebration was in full swing outside the ship as Deann led Dor into the captain's cabin and secured the door behind them. "Just be gentle with me," he grinned. She grabbed him and whipped him through the air. He landed on the bed with her astride him. She kissed him passionately, but he was gentle and pulled her down beside him. "Easy girl, it's all right." He pulled her onto his shoulder and smoothed her hair with a big hand.

"Dor?"

"It's all right, Dee."

"Saw through me, huh?"

"Yeah, I did."

"Dor ..." She got no further as great wracking sobs shook her frame and he held her close, cooing soothing sounds. He was still holding her when the emotional storm passed. "Dor, I ..."

"Hush now, I understand. You need time to mourn the loss of your lover."

Deann gave a great shudder then sighed. "I've had a year to mourn, but wouldn't face it. No, the time for that has passed and now it's time to move on." She brushed the hair back from his eyes then kissed him again. This kiss was softer and more loving. He returned it eagerly.

Deann lay still, her head pillowed on his chest, listening to him sleep. He'd been gentle, yet he had aroused the dormant passions in her. "Forgive me, Chella. I need this, my people need this. I hope you find someone to love too." She felt him stir then. "Awake?"

"Getting there," he replied sleepily. "Is it time for morning shift yet?"

"Not quite."

"Are you all right, Dee?"

"I'll be walking funny for a few days, but I'll manage."

He chuckled at that. "Yep, me too."

"Dor, there's something we should talk about."

"As your bonded companion, people will look to me for direction and favor when you're not around?"

"That and should anything happen to me, you'll be the one they turn to."

"Nothing will happen to you, or I'll be seriously unhappy."

"Fool," she chuckled, as she poked him in the ribs, eliciting a grunt. "I mean it. You'll have to learn everything you can about the ships, how they run, what stations ..."

"I get it, Dee. I'll do my best. I know what you mean, and I know what it means to be the Chieftain's companion."

"Oh?"

"My mother was chieftain's companion before the Iron Emperor came. This is a much smaller scale, but the working parts are the same. I won't let you down."

"I know you won't, Dor. I'm just fussing. You know how I like everything perfect."

"Always be prepared, then no matter what happens, you're ready. That was supposed to be your favorite saying according to the scholars. I've been waiting to hear it."

"It's a great motto, but ... My favorite saying?"

"Yes. Imagine my dismay to learn your most used saying is skeeter." She gave a shriek of protest then leaped on him and kissed him deeply. They were still slightly disheveled when the morning klaxon sounded.

There was lots of good-natured teasing and banter until exercises and training got underway. Later, as they gathered around a meal, Deann looked thoughtful. "You all right, Dee?" asked Barah. "Old Dor didn't wear you out, did he?"

Deann's eyes snapped into focus and he flinched. A smile played at the edges of her mouth for a moment. "Nellie, control your man."

"Yes, ma'am," Nellie replied, a twinkle in her eye. Barah suddenly lifted up into the air, floated over beside Nellie, then was set back down. "Behave." He grinned and kissed her cheek.

Pally's deep rumble was next. "Dee, what's going on in that head of yours?"

"I'm tired of all this waiting and I'm itching to get on the move. We need to do something, anything, before we rust in place. Dor, find Girta and Quint, Eddan too. We need to get organized." He rose to his feet and trotted off. Eddan soon appeared, chatting easily with a tall, red-haired woman. Dor and Quint soon followed.

"Gang's all here, Dee," said Barah. "What's up?"

"We need to know where we stand right now," replied Deann. "Pally, report. What's the readiness of the ships?"

"Three ships are functional. Two we've pillaged for parts and fuel. Of the three, the Raptor and the Dragon are battle ready. I'd hold the Comet back, she's in the worst shape."

"Small fighters?"

"Ten to a ship, but all are low on fuel and munitions. We've rigged everything we've got with inertial dampeners."

"Crew status?"

"We can crew two ships with full crew, everybody has been trained as best we can."

"Crew recommendations?"

"Your ship's the Raptor, Quint's is the Dragon, and Girta should command the Comet."

"Belay that," said Quint. "Girta was ever a more able Captain than I am in battle. I say we give the Dragon to Girta, I serve as first man, and Eddan flies the Comet with the elders, mothers, and children."

"You were chieftain, Quint. Now you're willing to settle for first man?" asked Deann.

"I became chieftain because Girta turned it down."

"I'd just lost my companion and son. I was in a bad place, you know, in my mind. Quint was still functional," said Girta.

Deanna nodded. "Barah, how's the fuel in our fighter?"

"We're down to about half and we've used up the spare rods. Weapons are working but we're down a bit on munitions."

"How are we for pilots?"

"We've got plenty; a dozen good ones. I've been working them with the dampeners on for a while now. We're good for pilots."

"Alise, how are we doing with spears and bows?"

"Many of the people are good with the spears, Captain Deann. "A few have taken to the bow as well. We hunt with bow and spear only now."

Deann gave her a nod of approval. "Before we stopped the mapping, did you ever see any life on any of the other levels?"

"No," replied Alise. "Most are empty, the few just below us have been taken over by forest, and the two above are empty. They look like they were living quarters, but they're empty of life."

"So, as far as we know, this level is the only one that has mobile life forms?" Alise nodded her agreement.

"Okay, Quint, when you folks fought the emperor, was it on this level?"

"Yes, we chased a few of his returning fighters back in."

"Was that far from here?"

"Yes. It was up ahead a long way. What are you thinking?"

"Stay with me now," she grinned. "If you were an emperor directing a battle, where would you be?"

"On the bridge of my ship," said Girta.

"Exactly," agreed Deann." Quint, when the emperor first appeared to fight, which direction did he come from?" Did he arrive in a transport or on foot?"

The light of understanding came into Quint's eyes. "He was on foot. Give me a minute... Girta?"

"We came through," said Girta, her eyes closed. Slowly she turned to face away, looking ahead into the great ship. "We burst through then turned the ships away from where we are now because the resistance was from the other direction. We faced heavy opposition, but were cutting our way through them when the emperor arrived and started knocking down our ships. He was shooting energy beams from his hands." She opened her eyes and spun back to Deann. "The bridge is that way."

"Now we're getting somewhere," grinned Deann. "Let's move on then. Describe the ships you fought."

"They were a bit bigger than ours, but slower," replied Quint. "It was the sheer number of them that gave them the victory."

"Did you ever get a look at who was flying them?"

"What??? No, no. I guess we just assumed it was the Tangles. You don't think so?"

"No I don't," replied Deann. "In the past year we've beaten them dozens of times, yet they keep on coming. Never any new tactics, never any new weapons. Why do you think that is?"

"They're wearing us down," said Barah. "Somebody else is sending them at us to use up our munitions."

"That was my thought," said Deann.

"So where does that leave us?" asked Quint.

"In a better place than we were," replied Deann. "We know we have a smarter enemy up ahead. I wonder ... Alise, find Leen for me."

Alise put two fingers in her mouth, tight to her tusks, then blew a loud, long, whistle. Instantly, Leen popped out of the Raptor and raced to them. She was smiling and fairly bouncing with excitement. She looked swiftly from one to the other in anticipation. Deann grinned as she spoke. "Leen, you sure are a ray of sunshine. Tell me, did you ever see any other people on this ship besides Red Nova and the Tangles?"

Leen's joy vanished instantly and her eyes were downcast. "Why?" She had long since mastered the language and rarely stopped chattering.

Deann reached out and tipped her chin up. "It's all right, Leen. You're safe here. Tell me of the others."

"I was too young to serve them, so I was given to the Tangles. The Tangles are slaves who were once slave masters in a faraway place. When their whips are turned down they burn but don't kill. They turn them up to use as killing weapons in battle."

"So the Tangles serve others. Who or what do they serve?"

"They serve the masters who fly the ships. I remember even though I was small."

Deann grinned. Leen never forgot anything, ever. "What do these masters look like?"

"They're tall, like Red Novans. They have seven fingers on each hand, they have two eyes, they have big heads with almost no ears. They move very quickly and are always fiddling with things with their hands."

"Fiddling?"

"Equipment, adjusting, checking, more adjusting, more checking."

"Are there many of them?"

"I don't know. I was only brought to them once. A wounded one was dying. I tried to help the older healer, but she whispered for me not to. The master died then they killed the healer. They gave me to the Tangles who used me for a healer. That was many years ago, after the coming of Red Nova. The Tangles don't like Red Novans. The masters say go kill Red Novans, but Red Novans are hard to kill so many Tangles die trying." Leen was getting her chatter back. "Please, Chieftain, don't send me back to them. I know I'm old enough to serve the masters now, but ..."

"Oh no, my girl," said Deann. "You're not going anywhere. You're the healer on my crew, my clan. You're staying right here with us. Go on back to the ship now and make sure that infirmary is ready for action." With a squeal of delight Leen hopped to her feet and sped away.

"She was afraid you would send her back," mused Alise.

"Why would she think that?"

"Leen has never known freedom until we found her. She's a creature of pure joy. It's only with Red Nova she's been allowed to express that, and it's increasing her healing powers. She told me that the Tangles would promise her she could serve the masters if she was good enough, but they always lied. We're the first she has even known who kept their word to her."

"Poor girl," mused Deann. "All right, back to business. The masters are out there trying to use up our ammo. Why?"

"They're afraid of us," grinned Dor. "Most of the Emperor's fleet was outside the ship for the battle. All his fighting ships. There were probably only a few essential crew left on board this monster, and they weren't combat troops. I'd say the Tangles were the ground troops, the masters were flight crews and fighter pilots, as well as big ship's crew. I'd also bet we knocked down most of them before we fought the emperor. I think we outnumber them."

"All right, where are they, Dor?" asked Deann.

"They're on the bridge," he replied with a huge grin. "Let's go get 'em."

"You sure that's the right course of action?" asked Deann, a twinkle in her eye.

"Got in a hurry, did I?" He shook his head then thought for a minute. "All right, they're on the bridge, that means they're the ones keeping the ship running. They should be the last on our list before we leave the ship. Fair enough. So the question now is, are we ready? Dee, I can see by the look on your face I've missed something."

"I think we all missed it," said Pally. "Come on, Captain, what did we miss?"

"We could make a run at it now," said Deann. "However, if we hit heavy resistance, we'd be out of fuel and munitions before we managed to reach the bridge."

"So, what's the answer?" asked Dor.

Deann thought for a moment then grinned. "Opinions? Options?"

"I say we go for it," said Quint. "A slim chance is better than no chance at all."

"Hold on," said Girta. "Look, the Tangles are being sent to use up our ammo and resources. Why? They're afraid of us. All right, why are they only sending small parties at us when they don't go back?"

"They're afraid," said Nellie. "They're not warriors, they're ship's crew, techies. They're terrified so they hold most of their people back to defend them in case we go after them. If we go at them we could find ourselves facing hundreds of Tangles, maybe thousands. We could defeat them, but only with our ships and that would deplete our resources too much. Am I right?"

"I think you're right, Priestess," said Girta. "Chieftain, I recommend we see if we can top up our weapons and fuel before we try this." There was a round of agreement from the others.

Deann nodded her agreement as well. "Do you know what their ships were using for fuel?"

"Same as us, I imagine," said Quint. "I remember them cleaning out the fuel dumps on Arcalia. We needed that fuel, but they beat us to it."

"All right then," said Deann, a smile on her face. "They would need to store fuel on this ship. We need to find that. Also, if there are any of their fighting ships still aboard, we need to locate and pillage those as well. We've been on the defensive too long. It's time we took over this damn ship, it's time to go on the attack.

"Alise, take your crew and see if you can locate the extra fuel. It'll probably be guarded. Don't try to do anything, just locate it."

"My crew, Chieftain?"

"You're chief hunter. Choose your crew and get it done."

"Yes, ma'am," grinned Alise, as she rose gracefully to her feet. "Dor, Barah, you're with me."

"Want a gunner?" asked Nellie.

"You would be a most welcome addition, Priestess Nellie. Let's go."

As they sped away to the small fighter ship, Deann sighed and rubbed her eyes. "Pally, I don't care what the nine hells you have to do, but get our damn comms back online."

"Yes, ma'am," he grinned, as he rose and headed back to the Raptor.

"Girta, get your ship crewed and ready. Rob every small fighter you have to make one or two ready for battle and get the best crew aboard it you can."

The tall woman grinned and rose to her feet. "Come on, First Man, we have our orders." Quint grinned and followed her.

Eddan sighed and gave Deann the *look*. "What?" she asked.

"Me, captain a ship? A helpless ship at that?"

"Eddan, here's the plan for once we get out of this damned monster. We'll have to find a planet where we can survive. We'll be a bit cramped if we take only two ships. If we take three we can spread out a bit. Hells, if I had the option I'd take all five. Once we find a planet we'll set up much as we are here. Your ship will then become the school, the nursery, the center of learning for all. I want every child born to the clan to be learning as much as possible as soon as possible. If the children are born to learning they'll think it the most natural thing in the world to do."

"What's going through that head of yours, Chieftain?"

"At any time in their history, did any of the Novans ever build their own ships?"

"Not that I'm aware of. The Arcalians supplied us at first. When Arcalia fell we raided the Imperial side of the Gap. Some ships we bought, some we stole, others we traded for. That was our weakness, wasn't it? We focused too much on fighting and became dependent for ships."

"No, you lost Blue Nova. You see, it's those artistic type folk who could help the engineers envision better ways of doing things. Once we get out of here, if we can find any remnants of the Blue clan ..."

"I begin to see why you were so adamant about educating every member of the clan."

"Knowledge is power, Eddan. The more we know, the better we can defend ourselves. The better we can make life for everybody in the clan."

"I'm in awe, Matriarch. I'll go see to preparing my ship now."

Deann smiled as he walked away. She rose and began her daily exercises. She was stiffer than she had expected to be. A smile crossed her face as she thought of the delights she experienced the night before. She had to admit it to herself, she was truly a sensual creature and Dor was a good match for her.

Preparing for War

It took weeks, but Alise found what she was looking for. A gigantic warehouse of fuel storage. The fuel rods weren't compatible, but they were close. With a bit of effort, they could be retooled to fit. They brought back as many as they could carry. It took Pally another month to retool the fuel rods, but once it was done they were able to put two small fighters in the air, fully fueled. Those two ferried back as much fuel as they could.

It was a painfully slow process. From the time they discovered the fuel to when they had all three ships topped up, and all the small fighters as well, another two years had passed. During that time both Deann and Alise gave birth and Nellie was heavy with child. Dor proved to be both a gentle lover and a doting father. He became an able leader as well and was promoted to First Man on Deann's ship, much to Pally's delight. Once again, he was chief engineer and happy to be so.

A number of the other women had given birth as well. Leen appointed herself chief nanny and set up a nursery on Eddan's ship. For the first time since the battle that trapped them inside the time ship, the Red Novans were well fed and hopeful. Their ships were fully fueled and they had the Matriarch to lead them. They were getting excited, but Deann was worried.

Pally found Deann beneath her favorite tree. Passing her a container of water, he sank to the ground beside her. Deann sighed as she accepted the water and took a sip. "Now what's broken down?"

"Number two water condenser."

"Skeeter, can you fix it?"

"I can. You wanted to see me?"

"How did you know?"

"Nellie told me."

"Some days that girl knows what I'm thinking before I do," said Deann. "Pally, the clan is growing. If we don't get off this damn time ship soon we'll need a fourth ship."

"I was afraid you'd say that. Dee, we pillaged the two ships to make three, well, two and a half. Look, to get another ship we'd have to find where they repaired the damages to their fleet, then I'd need a year or two to figure out how to fix one and make it usable for us. That's a couple of years we can't spare."

"I'm open to suggestions."

"We're fueled up, we could take a shot at it."

"All right, say we attack and defeat the opposition, gain the bridge. The enemy is scattered and we're in control. What then?"

"I spend another thirty years trying to figure out how to work the damn ship because we used up all our ordinance during the battle. We have nothing left to shoot our way out with. So what's the alternative?"

"Alise found us fuel we could use."

"You think she might find us weapons?"

"Yeah, I do," grunted Deann, as she squirmed a bit to get the baby attached to her nipple. He began to suckle noisily, and she returned to the conversation. "We need weapons now, Pally. Thing is, even if Alise finds them, ..."

"Can I adapt them to our needs, is that it?"

"Honest opinion, Pally, Do you think you can do it?"

"I won't know until I try, but I'd love to take a crack at it."

"There's one more thing. Keep this between us for now."

"Of course. Dee, what is it?"

"Why is this gods forsaken ship still here in the Gap? Why the hells haven't they tried to go home. They have the bridge, the ship is still running."

"There could be any of a hundred reasons. Dee..."

"Suppose it was Micha who had been sucked out the airlock. Wouldn't you try to retrieve him if you could?"

"Sure, but what... oh dear gods and magic. Skeet, Dee. You think they retrieved him?"

"They had control of the ship. They drove the Novans back. And the damn ship has stayed in the Gap. I wouldn't discount it. Think about it, they were a hundred generations after us, yet the damn thing appeared in our time."

"He's on board and hunting for Micha. This isn't good, Dee. If you're right we're in a heap of trouble."

"Pally, correct me if I'm wrong, but didn't your father make a third remote just in case?"

"He made three. That's why Lady Arlessa gave one away to that spy woman. The Lady has another for back up, so does Micha."

"Are they hard to make?"

A wide grin crossed his face. "Not at all. If you know the frequency, and I do. It's a low level frequency that would rarely if ever be used. In fact, I'll bet Dad put the how to in his engineer's manual."

"He wrote a manual?"

"Yeah, he gave it to me in case I hit something unusual on the Warbird. I've got it with me."

"You brought it with you?"

"We were exploring an unknown ship. Of course I brought it with me."

"Bless you, my friend. You're the best. Make up a dozen or so of those controllers just in case, would you?"

"Consider it done, Chieftain."

"Now, back to weapons. I highly doubt we'll find ordinance that will be useful, but what about energy beam weapons?"

"We've got them, both small arms and ship mounts, but we're desperate for energy cells. Ours are nearly depleted from running our daily needs. If we can find those it should be easy enough to adapt them."

"Still no comms?"

"We'll have short range and ship-to-ship by the end of day, but no long range yet."

"Do what you can, Pally. Any word from Alise yet?"

"No, and I'm starting to worry. It's been over a week."

"Yeah, me too."

"You've gotten pretty fond of old Dor, haven't you?"

Deann chuckled at the gentle teasing. "Yeah, I have, Pally. He's a good man."

"He's a good leader too, Dee. Everyone respects him. You chose well."

"Thanks Pally, that means a lot. I ..."

She got no further as two small fighters came in at speed and alit in the compound. Alise jumped out with Dor right behind her. She whistled for Leen who soon appeared. Dor started giving directions while Alise came to report. Deann had reached her feet in spite of the protest from her breast. She adjusted the baby to the other breast then stepped towards Alise.

"Alise, report."

"We found the place where they repair their damaged ships, Chieftain. Captain Deann, there are a number of damaged ships of familiar design. We believe they were trying to adapt them to their own needs.

"We tried to get a closer look, but were picked up on sensors. We had left our ships to gain greater stealth, but it wasn't enough. We fought our way back and escaped, but we have the location now. We have a few injuries, but nothing permanent and we lost no people."

"Well done, Alise." Deann peeked into the sling around Alise's body and smiled at the sleeping form hidden there. "Go find Pally now, then rest."

"Thank you, Chieftain." Alise smiled and withdrew.

Their discovery of the repair bays caused the enemy to add extra security. They were alert and waiting for another incursion. They weren't expecting what they got. Halfway back to the Raptor Deann's shoulder comm squawked. "Engineering to Captain Deann."

"Deann here."

"Comms are up, short range only, Captain."

"Well done, Engineering. Bridge."

"Bridge here," came the voice of a woman she knew as Tanie. The girl was smart and a good fighter, even if she was quite young.

"Tanie, warm up those engines and give me ship-to-ship."

"Ship-to-ship, aye," came the excited voice.

"Attention, all hands. Prepare for lift off."

There was a burst of excitement as people gathered what they could and hurried to their respective ships. Deann went by her infirmary to find Leen just finishing up with the wounded hunters. "Barah, you fit?"

"Fit and ready, Captain."

"Take pilot."

Leen reached towards Deann and Alise who had just appeared in the door. "Give then to me," she said. "Come on, give them to me. You can't be nursing on the bridge during a battle. Hand them over." Smiling shyly, the two young mothers handed over the babies then fled to the bridge.

Deann hopped into the captain's chair and Dor appeared at her right hand. Alise took weapons. Barah was at pilot and Nellie was on comms. "Ship-to-ship, Nellie."

"Ship-to-ship, aye."

"Attention all captains. We're going after that repair bay. We're expecting heavy resistance, but I don't believe they're expecting war ships. The Raptor will lead us in with the Dragon on her right flank. The Comet's not ready for a fight so she'll hold back a bit. Are we set?"

"Understood and set, Chieftain," came one reply and then the other. Eddan sounded nervous and Deann grinned.

"All right then, let's go hunting. Barah, is the course laid in and transmitted to the fleet?"

"Aye, Chieftain. Course laid in and transmitted."

"Take us up."

At that command, the Raptor lifted off the ground for the first time in over fifteen years. Deann's grin widened. She had a ship under her again and she suddenly felt alive. The three warships moved forward then dropped down a central shaft for three levels then turned forward again. An hour later Barah spoke again. "Approaching objective now, Captain."

Deann leaped to the sensor array. There were over two hundred lifeforms guarding what looked like a giant hangar. The sudden disarray among the defenders told her she'd been right. They hadn't anticipated the arrival of the war ships. "Fire!" The last of the hard ordinance streaked forward and exploded in the milling defenders obliterating half of them in a single salvo. Before they could recover or flee the Dragon opened fire.

The defenders were routed and fleeing in all directions. Two fighters dropped out of the Raptor and two more from the Dragon. While the great ships settled to the ground at the doors of the repair bay, the small fighters harried the fleeing Tangles. "Call them in before they get too far out of range," said Deann as she rose from the chair and left the bridge. Dor settled into the chair. "Comms, ship-to-fighters."

"Ship-to-fighters, aye," replied Nellie, using her sexy purr.

Dor chuckled and shook a finger at her. "Raptor to fighters."

"Fighter one, here."

"Two here."

"Come home, we're clear."

"Understood. Coming home."

Dor left the bridge and found Deann inside the hangar. She was hunting those who had tried to hide inside. There was a scattered resistance, but it melted away quickly. Most had fled through a series of side exits. Alise and several other hunters continued the search, but Deann stopped and began gazing around.

"This will be a nightmare to defend," said Dor.

"I know. Too many ways in and too many ways out. Did you recall the fighters?"

"It's done."

"Set them to watch and defend the ships while the rest of us explore."

"Stay in touch. Be careful."

She turned to him and he saw the fire in her eyes. She looked much as she had that first day he'd seen her. She gazed in his eyes for a moment then stepped into his arms and kissed him lightly. "I'll be careful, lover. Make sure I have a ship to come back to."

He chuckled, kissed her cheek, then returned to the ship. Deann went to join Pally and his engineering crews. "What's the good word?"

"Good word? We just used up all our ordinance and drained most of our batteries. If they come at us now we're doomed."

"That's what I love about you, Pally. You're just like Leen, always so upbeat." The other men snickered at that and Pally shook a finger at her.

"That's one of ours," he replied, pointing to a half gutted ship. "Go see what you can find, boys."

They trotted off and he turned to Deann. "Well, we scared the skeet out of them. I'd say we convinced them we're topped up and battle ready. Next time they come at us they'll mean it."

Just then there was a hoot of victory from the engineers. "Ammo. We've got ammo."

"Better to be lucky than good," grinned Deann as they set out to join the excited men. The ammunition from the gutted ship had been neatly piled beside it. The work benches beside it were loaded with parts that had been stripped off. Pally was grinning. "I'll just leave you to it. I'll be back on the Raptor feeding Dor's kid. Let me know how it's going."

"Understood." He was already back to her, inspecting some of the parts. Deann barely made it back to the ship before he came back on comms. "Pally to Deann."

"Go ahead, Pally."

"Dee, your gamble paid off big time. We've found another seven salvaged ships. We can top up our weapons and fully charge our energy storage. If you can keep them off me for a few weeks I'll give you three fully armed and battle ready ships."

"Understood." He could hear the excitement in her voice.

It wasn't to be as easy as all that. They were exposed and the enemy knew where to find them. They came in force. They even fielded one large fighting ship. Deann had scouts well out, so she had some warning, but there was no time to lose. The Raptor leaped into the air and sped to meet them head on. The refurbished ship, complete with new inertial dampeners performed above expectations.

The Raptor bore down on the enemy ship, twisting and turning as she avoided the enemy fire. Barah let out a whoop of pure joy as he guided the ship through the morass of enemy small fighters and the big ship's fire. Tanie and Elise were on guns and proved to be an effective team. They swept past the enemy ship then turned back for a second run. This time the enemy ship floundered and exploded.

Once again the Raptor turned and came in, this time concentrating all her fire on the massed ground troops, ignoring the two small fighter ships. As she passed overhead, raining destruction down on the enemy, the launch bay doors opened spilling out three small fighter ships. The enemy was horrified at the speed and agility of the smaller ships and soon they were down and the ground troops in full flight.

The Raptor returned to her guard station to find the Dragon in a battle with two enemy ships. She joined the fight and it was soon over.

This pattern was repeated every few days for several weeks. Pally was exhausted and so were his engineers. Every time a new battle raged, Tangles would appear through one door or another and try to retake the repair station. Pally and his crew weren't just trying to salvage what was available, but they were fighting a hard battle at the same time.

"Dammit, Dee, we're getting nowhere. Every time we top up the weapons and fuel they come at us again and use it up."

"I'm wide open to suggestions," she replied, a hard edge to her voice. Like most Novan ships, the mess hall had become the general meeting room. They were there, but the food was relatively untouched. "Anybody else got any more bad news?"

"We're running low on food again." Came a soft apologetic voice from the kitchen.

"Great." Deann sighed then shook her head. She rose and began to pace. No one disturbed her while she thought her way through the mess they were in. Finally she stopped and turned back to her chair. She slumped into it. "All right, we're beating the snot out of them and we're losing. I hate that. We need to change tactics a bit. Pally, do you know where the supplies are that you need?"

"Yes, but we need to be left alone to gather them and we need to not be using them up the instant we get them."

"Understood. Alise."

"Yes, Captain Deann?"

"Where's the nearest forest where we can gather food?"

"Not far, half an hour to the central shaft then one level up. There was plenty of animal life, but no human or enemy."

"Good. Take your crew of hunters and find us a place there where we can hide all our ships."

"On it, Chieftain. Dor, Barah, Tanie."

"And me?" asked Nellie.

"And you, little mother," smiled Alise, as Nellie adjusted the sling that held her baby. "Let's go people."

"So, what's the plan, Chieftain?" asked Girta.

"We establish a new compound. Let them have this place for now. We catch a rest, top up our food supplies then we change the game. We stop being the target and we make them the target. Pally, get everything aboard the ships you can. I'll want at least six small fighters prepped for battle and when we get set up in the new compound I want the Comet gutted for a freighter. We'll raid these bastards, steal the supplies we need then vanish. They can't use up our supplies if they can't find us."

Pally chuckled, the first smile in days coming to his eyes. "I like it, Dee. We've caught a breather right now, I'll take the guys and load as much as I can find onto the ships. As soon as Alise gets back we'll be ready to go."

"Do it, Pally. Take as many men as you need. Don't waste any time, just grab whatever looks like it might be useful; you can sort it out later." He nodded and left the table.

"What do you think, Girta?"

"I like it, Deann. We'll lose fewer people this way. I have to say, with all the training we've been doing these past few years we're a lot more efficient and successful than we ever were before. Now, while the boys are loading up the ships, why don't you go play with the kids for a bit before they start thinking Leen is their mother."

"Yes, ma'am," Deann sighed elaborately then grinned. She rose and headed off to the nursery. Both of the warships had a nursery now and the Comet was carrying only supplies. Deann wanted to make it a full battleship as well, if she could. She was mulling this over in her mind as she reached the nursery.

"Mamma!" The voice was followed by a child climbing nimbly up her leg. With a laugh of delight she scooped him into her arms. "Well now, how's my fierce warrior today?"

Deann wrestled with him and played until he fell asleep in her arms, cuddled up to his younger sister. Leen was fussing with something and chatting away as usual. "Leen?"

"Yes, Chieftain Deann?"

"It just occurred to me. Are there others like you on the big ship? Do you know?"

"Before I was given to the Tangles I was kept with five others, all young like me. There were also three elders that I was aware of. I have seen no others of my kind for many long years. Why do you ask?"

"Just wondering."

"Dee?"

"If we get back to my time, and I now have hopes that we will do just that, Alise will have three others like her. I believe it's important for a person to see others like herself from time to time."

"So they don't feel so alone. I understand, but I'm not alone, Dee. I'm Red Novan and there are many of us." She stopped and looked wistful for a moment. "It would be nice to see another Eldin face though."

"Eldin, is that what your people are called?"

"Yes. My mother told me before I was taken away."

"Your mother? She's on this ship?"

"No, not for many years. She was the one who told me not to cure the master."

"And they killed her. Leen, I'm sorry for that."

"Don't be, Chieftain Dee. I'm happy here. I have a good life and many people who like me. I get to play with the youngsters, heal the sick and wounded, I'm well fed, and I'm content."

"Still, we'll keep an eye out for another Eldin." Gently, Deann rose and deposited the sleeping children on the bedding Leen had placed on the floor. "We could use another healer or two for the other ships," she mused, as she returned to the bridge.

Two days later the ships were topped up and Alise returned with another attack force right on her heels. The Novan ships fled, and the enemy reclaimed the hangar. Three weeks later the Novans returned. The Raptor came in fast and low, did a lot of damage with energy weapons only, and then fled with the enemy in close pursuit. The Raptor was faster and more agile so it was relatively easy to stay just out of the line of fire.

After leading the enemy a merry chase for a while, the Raptor just seemed to vanish. She turned into the path of her pursuers and shot past. Before the enemy could manage the turn the Raptor vanished into the central shaft. All attempts to find her proved fruitless. The Comet was already waiting at the new compound when the Raptor returned.

"Well, how did we do?" asked Deann, as she bounded out of the ship and approached the Comet where a full crew were unloading the ill-gotten gains.

"Better than I'd hoped," replied Pally. "We got enough fuel and munitions to top you up and bring the Dragon near to full as well."

"Perfect. Lots of spare parts?"

"Not so much. We were focused on fuel and munitions. What's on your mind, Dee?"

"I'd like to get the Comet battle ready too if we can."

"We'll need to do a few more raids to make that happen, Dee." Pally sighed. "Do you really think that's necessary? What's going through your head now?"

She lowered her voice so only he could hear. "Did you ever get time to make those remotes to stop the robot?"

"Not yet."

"Make the time, Pally."

"Dee?"

"This ship is still in the Gap, in our time. I'd bet my life on it. He came back to get another crack at Micha. The odds are that he's still commanding this ship ..."

"And if he is, then he'll hold her steady in our proper time, where he knows Micha is."

"Right."

"So, when we break out of here we'll come out right when we left?"

"Give or take a few years or so, yeah, I think so. That's what that energy field around the great ship was about."

"Time distortion."

"Exactly, Pally my friend. That's why our comms wouldn't work. We tried to report to the Warbird, but were already in a different time."

"Of course, time distortion. Dee, I think I can get full comms back."

"Seriously? Oh man, that would be so awesome. What's the key?"

"Time distortion, Dee. Remember we always had to re-calibrate the comms every two years?"

"Yeah, so?"

"So, in here we're probably ten to twenty years out of sync. Should have everything back to norm in a jiffy."

"Do it, Pally. Get those remotes ready too, top priority."

"Right you are, Chieftain. Nothing to it. Fix the comms, make the magic remotes, create a battleship, ..."

"Stop whining and start working," said Deann. They were both laughing as she pushed him towards the growing pile of salvage that was being off loaded from the Comet.

As Deann walked back towards the Raptor she was smiling, yet her mind was still racing ahead. "Soon we'll have three ships fully topped up and ready. It'll then be time to attack the bridge. We're one more step closer to getting home."

The Bridge

The scene before Deann's eyes cut through her heart, and like daggers laid her soul bare and bleeding. Tears leaked from her eyes and her whole body trembled as the carnage played out before her. Ships cut apart, crashing to the surface, people fleeing only to be cut down, flayed alive by the Tangle Troops, their bodies stripped of flesh even as they screamed.

"Chieftain?" The lights came up and the screen went blank.

Deann shook off the emotion, angrily brushing the tears off her cheeks. "Eddan, what was that?"

"Forgive me, Chieftain. I didn't mean to leave that lying around. It's just something I'm working on as an historian. Did you want to see me for something?"

"First answer the question. What was that, fact or fiction?"

Eddan sighed and slumped into a chair. They were in his tiny workshop as he called it. Absent mindedly, he reached for a container of water and passed it to her then got one for himself. "It was fact. What you saw was something I put together from the flight recorders and personal recorders of our ships and fighters."

"So what was it?"

"The fall of Arcalia. Red Nova tried to save it because we needed the fuel and munitions, not to mention the billions of humans there. We failed and were driven back. I'll destroy that if you wish. It was just a way to keep my mind occupied over the years."

"No, keep it. Better yet, make me a copy."

"Why, Chieftain?"

"To remind me that we have to make things different this time."

"This time?"

"This time. Actually, I forgot why I came here in the first place. Find Quint and Girta then meet me in the Raptor, the meeting room."

She was still badly shaken as she walked away towards her own ship. Reaching for her newly functional comms, she began to call her council to her. "Nellie, Alise, Dor, Barah, Quint, Girta, Tanie, meeting room on the Raptor. Now."

They gathered round a table waiting for Deann to speak. Her mind was in a whirl, but she got control of it. She nodded at Eddan who set up a small vid screen and let the fall of Arcalia play for a few moments. Quint and Girta were the only ones besides Eddan who'd been there. He let it play for a few moments, then at her signal stopped it. They all were shaken by the sheer brutality of it.

"That, people, is the enemy we face. That will be our fate and the fate of our people should we fail. Now I'll tell you who that enemy is. We face the Iron Emperor himself. We'll face him on the bridge, then we'll leave this accursed ship. When we do we'll be in our own time. We'll take steps to make certain this never happens."

"Chieftain, the emperor was blown out the air lock," said Eddan.

"I believe they retrieved him. Why else did this ship appear in my time rather than go home to its own galaxy? What could make these people, these slave masters, remain so far from home when the man who conquered them was dead? No, they brought him back inside. They woke him up, but I believe he's damaged, that's why they haven't actually make a move on Micha yet."

"Micha?" asked Eddan. "The founder of Gold Nova?"

"Yes," replied Deann, "and the emperor's rival, his enemy. Twice they fought, and twice Micha beat him. He came back to this galaxy for revenge. That's why I believe he's holding the ship here. We're in a time field, but make no mistake, when we leave we'll be in my time."

"So, why hasn't he come at us harder?" asked Barah.

"He doesn't know we're here. Oh, he knows Red Nova has a few refugees on the ship, but I'll bet he has no idea at all that the five of us are here. If he did he'd have come for Nellie in a heartbeat."

"Why Nellie?" asked Dor.

"I'm his granddaughter," replied Nellie. Her tiny fists were clenched, and a cold fire played about her hands. The look in her eyes spoke of death and worse. "Believe me when I say," she said, pointing at the vid screen, "I will never allow that to happen."

"Skeet," muttered Girta. "How do we defeat him? If it is him, how do we stop him when our whole fleet couldn't even slow him down?"

"With these," replied Pally, as he began passing out small hand held remote controllers.

"Grandfather was dying," explained Nellie. "He had a robotic body built and his brain implanted in it. However, the man who built it didn't trust him completely. He built in a safety control. The red switch here will freeze the emperor's body and put his mind to sleep. He's tried to get the chip removed from his brain, but it grows back. The man who built him is dead, killed by Pally's mother. Rathbone discovered these controllers and gave Pally the instructions to build more. You have to get close to him to use it, but it should work."

"Should work," said Quint. "I'd rather not be close to him if it doesn't."

"If it doesn't," replied Nellie, "I'll deal with him myself. My grandfather died before I was born. That robotic abomination is no kin of mine, and I will not allow it to live. Dee, you know why Micha failed to stop him completely, don't you?"

"He did it for your mother. He allowed the robot to continue to exist so in her mind a piece of her father would still be out there somewhere. I swear to you, Nellie, I'll be guided by no such compassion. Once we catch that damn thing I'm sending it into the heart of the first sun I find." She waved her hand at the vid screen. "This will not be allowed to happen.

"Now, Eddan, tell me exactly when Arcalia fell the first time. When did King Borad die?"

"Well, it was after your children were born. As I recall, according to the chronicles, you were celebrating the second birthday of your youngest when you got the word."

"Skeeter, we're out of time. Chel is already past one year. Pally, how close are we to being ready?"

"We've topped up the Raptor and the Dragon, shields are at full capacity on all three and we're good for fuel. Sadly, our munitions aren't up to full and the Comet only has energy beams. All storage batteries are up to max though. Do you want to make another raid first?"

Again Deann motioned at the vid screen. "We're out of time, people. At first shift tomorrow we go for the bridge. We're getting off this damned abomination of a time ship. I've been here well over six years and that's long enough. Get some rest. Tomorrow Red Nova goes to war."

They dispersed, each thinking about what they'd learned and what was about to happen. There was lots of excitement as the word spread through the clan that tomorrow was the big day. Dor quietly followed Deann back to the bridge. "Have you got a plan to take the bridge?" he asked softly, as she settled into the captain's chair.

"We'll go right at them, batter them aside until we get close, that's when he'll come out swinging. I'll be in a small fighter with Nellie. As soon as he shows up she'll get his attention and I can get close enough to freeze him. As soon as he's out of the game the rest will fall easily."

"I sure hope you're right, girl."

"Trust me." The wolfish snarl on her face made him shiver and he knew he'd far rather face the Iron Emperor in battle than his own wife.

Not many people got a lot of sleep that night. When the morning klaxon sounded all were ready and at their posts. Deann appeared and settled into the captain's chair. "Comms, ship wide."

"Ship wide, aye Chieftain." A young woman, still in her teens, was at the comms. Her excitement was easy to read in her voice.

"Attention, all hands, we're going into battle as soon as we find the bridge or whatever defends it. You all have your assignments. Today we regain our freedom. Battle stations. Comms, ship-to-ship."

"Ship-to-ship, aye."

"Girta, Eddan, are you ready?"

"Dragon ready, Chieftain," came Girta's voice.

"Comet ready, Chieftain. Quint commanding."

"Where's Eddan?"

"Right here, Chieftain," he said as he stepped before the view screen. "You need an experienced captain at the helm of this ship, Chieftain. Quint is by far the better man for the task."

Deann gazed at him for a moment then spoke. "Understood and accepted. Barah, get us in the air."

The Raptor leaped up followed closely by her sister ships. They swept into the central shaft, rose to the main level then swung towards the front of the time ship. A half hour later they picked up the defenses on sensors. "Dee, they've massed in one spot, more are coming."

"How many ships do we face?"

"Seven."

Deann grinned for a moment. "Are they ever in for a surprise. Gunner?"

"Ready, Captain Deann," replied Alise.

"Good. Now let's go hunting. Ship to ship."

"Ship to ship, aye. Go ahead, Chieftain."

"Dragon on my right, Comet take the left flank. Remember Arcalia, people. We will not retreat, we will not surrender, and we will take no prisoners. Death to the Tangles."

A cry of "Death to the Tangles!" rang through all three ships just before the Raptor slammed into the defenses. Alise fired, then Barah rolled the ship aside so all return fire missed. The inertial dampeners were working perfectly. Alise fired on the second ship scoring a direct hit. It crashed as did two more brought down by the Dragon. The Comet accounted for another, but it was harder going with only energy beams.

The massed Tangles below tried to flee, but we driven back to their position by some unknown force. It was the slave collars. Even the masters who wielded the whips wore the pain collars. It was now two clumsy ships against the three faster and more agile Novan ships. In mere moments they were down and burning.

The three predators regrouped then made a run right at the masses of Tangle troops. They scattered in all directions. As the Tangles scattered the three ships opened up and several small fighter ships dropped out. These small ships darted in and out of the mass melee. The area was nearly free of Tangles when an energy beam struck one of the fighter ships exploding it completely. The Emperor had arrived.

His next several attempts failed as the ships were too agile and fast. He was getting frustrated when one small ship landed almost in front of him. He sent a blast of energy at it, but it was brushed aside. Nellie stepped out of the fighter and, her black robes wreathed in flames, strode out to face him. "Hello again, Grandfather." That cold voice carried well and he stopped, tilting his head to look more closely at her. The rest of the fighter's crew had climbed down as well, but he ignored them.

"You're Nellie, Brenna's daughter." The rasping voice ground out the words; they could see the machine was struggling.

"Yes, I'm Nellie. Call off your troops. Let's talk."

The machine shifted slowly. Obviously movement was difficult for it. A wave of its hand and the tall creatures near began tapping frantically at the tablets in their hands. All remaining Tangle troops in the area stopped moving and stood still. The Dragon and the Comet settled to the ground, but no one came out. "Come closer, child. Let me see you. Lower your shield, I won't harm you."

Nellie walked closer, allowing the flames surrounding her to die down. She stepped slightly to her right as she approached him. He turned with her, painfully slow. He paid no attention at all to Deann. The Emperor reached toward the small witch then froze in place, his hand still inches away from her face. Tilting her head to look at him, Nellie ducked under his outstretched arm and knocked on his forehead with her knuckles. "Looks like it worked, Dee."

Deann was close enough to the emperor to touch him when she threw the switch. He froze instantly. "I believe you're right, Nellie. Okay, we're not finished yet. Keep your eye on him once I bring him back to life. I don't want to take any chances with this thing." Nellie nodded then stepped back, raising the shield around herself and Deann again.

Deann stepped closer to the man/machine. "Listen carefully, Emperor. You are my servant. You will obey my every command instantly." She gave it a minute to sink in then threw the switch to bring him back. Nellie was on full alert and both Barah and Alise were close, armed with remotes of their own just in case. Slowly the machine straightened up.

"Nellie? Where did you go so quickly?"

"Never mind that, Loran," said Deann. "I have a task for you."

"Command me, Mistress."

"Have your assistants take my people to where they can top up their weapons and fuel."

"At once, Mistress. You there, guide these people to the munitions and fuel stores." Wide-eyed, the many fingered creature bowed deeply then obeyed. He ran swiftly, but Pally caught him and hauled him into the Raptor. The ships rose into the air and flew off.

"Stand at attention and await my next instruction."

"Yes, Mistress Lizera." The machine came to attention with difficulty.

Nellie's voice sounded in Deann's mind. "He thinks you're that spy woman who was sent through with him. Play along." Deann nodded.

"Loran."

"Yes, Mistress?"

"Have these things bring all the Eldin to me here."

"At once, Mistress." He gestured with his hand and one of the tall creatures came to him. He touched the object in the thing's hand and a voice jabbered out of it. The creature nodded then dashed away. A while later it reappeared with seven Eldin, three adults and four adolescents. They seemed confused as they knelt before the emperor.

An hour later the ships returned. There had been a fuss at the fuel dump, but with the shouted instruction from the Emperor's minion and a few well-placed shots from Alise's gun they got the idea. All three ships were topped up and fully armed.

No sooner was the Raptor on the ground than Deann was on the comms. "Leen, get out here now."

"Acknowledged. On my way." Leen soon appeared and approached fearfully. She was still uncertain.

Deann smiled at her to reassure her all was well. "Leen, take the Eldin to the sick bay on the Raptor. Fix them up then feed them. We'll all talk later." The girl came to life instantly, chattering away happily as she helped them to their feet and herded them off to the ship.

"Loran, can you open the launch bays from the bridge of my ship?"

"Of course, Mistress. May I ask where we're going?"

"I'm taking you to see the Witch's Hound again. Is that not why we came back?"

"Yes, yes it is. I came back to kill him, but I don't remember you on the voyage here." He froze in place and Deann sighed deeply.

"Didn't take him long to start wising up," grumbled Nellie. "What do you think, Dee?"

"Well, the off switch seems to be working." She stepped closer to the robot again. "Loran, you will obey my commands instantly and without question." She threw the switch again. "Loran, can you operate the time ship from the bridge of my ship?"

"I will need a command module." He gestured for one of the creatures to approach. Reluctantly it passed him the module in its hands.

"Come." Deann marched back to the Raptor, Loran walking awkwardly behind her. Barah and crew brought the fighter back on board. Deann reached for her comms. "All Red Novans back to their ships on the double. We're leaving the time ship."

There were fearful looks and deep surprise as Deann led the Iron Emperor onto the bridge. "Comms, ship wide."

"Ship wide, aye."

"Attention all personnel, we're leaving. Lock her down." She waited for a long moment then Pally's voice came over the comms. "All personnel accounted for and ship is secure, Captain."

"Acknowledged. Comms, ship-to-ship."

"Ship-to-ship, aye."

"Dragon, are you locked down and ready?"

"Dragon locked down and ready, Chieftain."

"Comet?"

"Comet locked down and ready, Chieftain."

"All right, Loran, open every launch bay and every air lock on the time ship."

"Mistress, that will kill everyone on the ship."

"I know. I don't care."

"Excellent thinking. This way the ship will still be here when we return for it. Wait, if we kill all of these who will fly it for us?"

"We'll bring more slaves. You can teach them what they need to know."

"Of course, Mistress. Opening launch bay doors and air locks now." His hand moved painfully over the command console, then they felt the ship waver slightly as all air rushed out into space, along with everything else that wasn't fastened down.

"Which way to the nearest launch bay?"

"Two levels down and to the left," replied the robot. "Mistress, how did you get here? I don't ..." He got no further as Deann deactivated him.

"Dor, get a couple of guys up here to put that damned robot into a cold storage bin."

"Why not just blow him out the air lock?"

"That's been tried. Didn't work. No, we're going to finish this robot's career forever. After I get done he's never coming back. Put him in storage."

"Aye, captain." Dor grinned and signaled another man to help him. Together they carried the robot off the bridge.

"What's the matter, Tanie?" asked Deann. "You were expecting a harder battle?"

The younger woman at the sensor panel just grinned sheepishly. "I guess I was. Matriarch, why did the robot obey you?"

"He can't help himself. The man who built him knew what he was building, an immortal and unstoppable machine, an indestructible conquering machine. He built in a failsafe, just in case. Once the emperor is frozen by the controller he's completely susceptible to the power of suggestion. That was his weakness. I believed if I could get close enough to shut him down I could make him let us go, help us to destroy the time ship."

"Well, it sure worked," said Pally, as he arrived on the bridge. "There's the launch bay doors and they're wide open. Oh, here's a little present for you Dee."

"What's this?"

"The two receiver chips from the emperor's skull. Without those he can't be revived."

"Wouldn't they grow back?"

"Not before we drop him in a sun somewhere." Deann grinned and nodded her thanks as the Raptor shot through the open launch bay doors followed closely by the Dragon and the Comet. A wild cheer sounded through every ship as they cleared the displacement field and flew into open space. Red Nova was free once again.

"We're clear of the distortion field, Captain."

"Barah, where are we?"

"Right where we're supposed to be, Captain," he replied from the pilot's station.

"When are we?"

"Unknown."

"Sensors, anybody in the area?"

"Nothing on sensors, Captain Deann," replied the girl at the sensor panel.

"All right, Barah, did you upload everything from the fighter we brought to the Raptor's central computer?"

"I did. Everything we had is there."

"All right, set a course for Arcalian space and transmit to the fleet. The ins and outs of the Gap will be different now than they were when these ships first flew."

"Understood. Course laid in and transmitting. We're good to go. Dee, we'll have to go around the time ship. We came out on the wrong side."

"Understood. Go around, but maintain a good distance. I don't want to get dragged back in there again."

"I heard that," grinned Barah.

He corrected his course then all three ships dipped well below the belly of the gigantic time ship. As they came up the other side and set out for Arcalian space, another ship appeared on sensors. "Chieftain, I have a ship on sensors."

Deann was on her feet in a heartbeat. "One ship?"

"Just one, Matriarch."

"Dee, do you think ..." said Barah.

"There's only one ship that should be here if we came out in the right place and time. That has to be the Warbird."

"We're being hailed."

"On visual."

"Approaching ships, you're trespassing in Nova Clan territory. Power down and identify or be destroyed." It was a very pregnant Michella looking at them.

"Belay that," said Deann, as she moved closer to the screen. "This is the Raptor, Deann of Red Nova commanding. Stand by, we're locking up with you."

A Difficult Reunion

Michella fought her way to the bridge, even though Alore begged her to return to the infirmary. Alore was deeply concerned. Michella should have given birth already and was struggling. Ellie rarely left her side anymore, especially since Deann's ship had disappeared into the energy field that surrounded that monstrous ship. With Alore at one elbow and Ellie at the other, Michella made it to the captain's chair. "Any sign?" she asked hopefully.

"None, Captain," Hawk replied gently.

"Captain, it's been two weeks. Perhaps we should find the rest of Nova clan and ..."

"No. We need to be here for Deann when she returns. We ..."

"Ships inbound. Three in all."

"What ships? Where?"

"Coming up from under the giant, Captain," replied Ellie, who had made a jump to the sensors.

"Shall I hail them, Captain?" asked Bim.

"Yes, hail them." Michella sat up straighter in the chair. She was waiting for the return of a small fighter, not a fleet of intruders this deep into the Gap. Dammit anyway. She was in no shape to fight a battle.

"Go ahead, Captain."

"Attention approaching ships, you're trespassing in Nova Clan territory. Power down and identify or be destroyed." She went into shock at the hard voice that responded. She knew that voice. It was her lover returned. She was so elated it took a moment for the message to sink in. Red Nova? Deann of Red Nova commanding? What the nine hells was going on? A sudden powerful contraction hit her before she could speak. She was vaguely aware that the voice was barking orders at her ship.

"Respond. Is this the Warbird? If not you have ten seconds to make peace with your maker."

Alore and Ellie leaped to assist Michella. Old Rath stepped to the vid screen. "This is the Warbird, Rathbone of Urn commanding. Please re-identify."

"Poppa Rath, it's Deann. Slow your rotation and lock us up now. I'll need Hawk on the bridge when I get there. I'm coming aboard."

Michella held out an arm towards the screen. "Wait ..."

"Dammit to the nine hells, there's no time for this. The Warbird is no match for the Raptor let alone all three ships. Now slow the rotation and lock up. Don't make me do this the hard way. Deann of Red Nova out."

Old Rath turned to Michella, but another contraction hit and she gasped. He turned back. "Slow the rotation, Pilot. Lock us up." Hawk nodded as his fingers flew across the controls. Within moments they felt the bump as the two ships locked together. A moment after that several heavily armed people burst onto the bridge, Barah and Nellie with them. Deann was barking orders.

"Barah, pilot. Hawk, this man is Eddan. Take him to the conference room, he has information for you. Eddan, stay on topic now, give him everything you have on the death of King Borad. Hawk, listen to this man and believe what he says, I'll explain all later. Go."

She shooed them away then a strange looking creature elbowed her way through to Michella, chattering the whole time. "Oops, sorry, out of the way. Make a hole. Move it. Healer coming through." She reached Michella and placed her hand on her abdomen. Michella felt instant relief. "Matriarch, this one is in trouble."

"Understood. Nellie, float Chella down to the infirmary. Alore, this is my healer, Leen. Work with her, she can do wonders for childbirth."

"How would you know, Miss Bossy?" Alore was confused and angry, as well as terrified for Michella.

"She helped me birth my two. Get moving. Sensors, has anything else come out of that monster?"

"No, Ma'am," replied the woman at the sensor panel.

"Good. Dor, get back to the Raptor and unhook us, we've got to get moving."

"You're not coming?"

The people on the bridge were surprised at the affection in her voice as she replied to him. "Not right now. I have to brief these folks, Leen needs a bit of time to help Chella, and we can't sit here while we wait. We have to be on the move. As soon as I've got everybody up to speed we'll lock up again and I'll come home."

"Aye, Captain."

Deann gripped his arm and gazed into his eyes. "Dor, I will come home." He nodded and trotted away. A short time later they felt the two ships unlock.

"Barah, Arcalian space, all possible speed."

"Aye, Chieftain, Arcalian space, all possible speed."

The Warbird shot away followed closely by the three Red Novan Ships. Deann spotted Ellie staring at her. She stepped over to the little witch and suddenly hugged her. "Gods I've missed you, Ellie, all of you folks."

"Dee, you were only gone two weeks," replied Ellie.

"Is that all it was out here?" she asked, as she released her friend.

"How long was it in there, Dee?" asked Old Rath.

"Somewhere between six and seven years," she replied heavily.

He nodded. "I thought you had a few more scars."

"Yeah, I do. I kept my word to you, though."

"Oh?"

"Yes. I promised to pass along what you taught me. I did that. There are fifty-seven able bodied warriors in Red Nova Clan and every one of them has been training by your methods for six years. They're a hard-headed and extremely dangerous clan. I want to introduce you to all of them. They'll probably blame you for me driving them so hard, but ..."

At that point Hawk came flying through the door. Deann stepped into his path. "This ship is headed for Arcalian space at all possible speed. You're on comms."

"Thank you."

"Take comms now, do what you do, there's no time to lose."

"Aye, Captain." Bim slid easily out of the way and Hawk sat to the console. His fingers flew for a while then he sighed and allowed his shoulder to relax. "Message sent, Captain."

"All right, Poppa Rath, bring Ellie, Hawk, Tarah, and everybody else you think should be in the know immediately, to the kitchen. I'll meet you there."

Deann left the bridge and slowly made her way to the infirmary. Of all the battles she had faced, this would be the hardest thing she had ever had to do. She arrived at the door to hear the voices inside. "Oh gods, the cord is around his neck, he's blue."

"Quickly, Alore, unwind the cord. Rest now, Michella, all is well. See, he's breathing easily now and his color is coming up nicely. My, he's a fine, strong boy."

Deann smiled as she listened to Leen chatter away, relieving everybody's tension and alleviating their fears. The baby started to scream lustily, and her smile broadened. Suddenly the screaming stopped and all she heard was a suckling sound, and then Leen's voice again. "You must rest now. Hold him gently and I'll remain here with you, as will Alore."

"You made her sleep," said Alore.

"Yes, sleep, yes. Healing goes faster in sleep. She will awaken renewed and ready to face the world once again."

"How did you do that? Are you a witch?"

"Witch, no. Not like Priestess Nellie. My kind do have some healing magic. Some we are born with and some we learn. I could teach you the learning things. We would have to ask permission of the Matriarch, but I'm sure she'll approve." Leen continued to chatter on and Deann slipped away to the mess hall. Michella was sleeping. She had a short reprieve.

She entered to find Nellie held tightly in Ellie's arms. Old Rath and Hawk were listening while Eddan talked. Eddan rose as she entered. "Matriarch, I've related to these men how you came to Red Nova, how Red Nova came to be, and how we escaped the time ship, as you instructed."

"Have you shown them the vid yet?"

"Not yet."

"Do it, Eddan." She sighed as she sank into a chair.

Eddan showed them a few moments of the vid. "The fall of Arcalia, as Red Nova experienced it," he said. Ellie was horrified as was Tarah. Old Rath and Hawk showed no emotion, but their hard eyes said it all. Eddan shut it off.

"That, people, is why I commandeered this ship and why we're in such a hurry to get to Arcalian space. If we can prevent the assassination of King Borad we may be able to prevent this. What you've just seem is the second fall of Arcalia, but as a direct result of the king's premature death none the less."

"You're different, Dee," said Ellie.

"I know, Ellie. I know. It is what it is and none of it could be helped. I didn't have a lot of choices."

"Did you speak to Chella yet?"

"She was a bit busy when I went down to the sick bay. I have no idea what his name will be, but Baby Blue has arrived right on schedule. Leen put her to sleep so she can heal. Right now Alore is picking Leen's brain for healing knowledge from a galaxy far away."

"You have to talk to her," said Ellie.

"Can't I just run away back to my ship?"

"No, you can't," said Nellie as she lightly slapped Deann's shoulder, "and you know it. What would the clan think? The fearsome Matriarch of Red Nova, running away like a frightened chicken?" Deann laughed and the others began to relax as Nellie's teasing took the tension out of the room.

"So, you trained all of them?" asked Rathbone.

"You have to understand," said Eddan. "We were defeated, broken, just waiting to die but stubbornly refusing to go quietly. Everything we had ever known, loved, or believed in was stripped away by those things you saw on the vid. The Borelian Clans annihilated, the Nova Clans, utterly destroyed; we were all that survived, and we didn't expect to last long. We'd been aboard that ship for twenty years, our number cut to half, and then she appeared.

"Out of legend the Matriarch came. She gave us hope, renewed our courage, built our strength, and led us against the foe. She became one of us, as did her companions, and together we defeated that which had destroyed everything in its path. She made us strong again." He sighed and looked at Deann with loving compassion. "And in so doing she gave up her own life, hopes, dreams, plans, to serve Red Nova."

Deann smiled and patted Eddan's arm. "It's been a good life, my friend. No, not the one I planned, but a good life. In life we take what comes to us and work with it, right Poppa Rath?"

"Indeed we do, Deann. I've got to say, I'm quite proud of you. So, what now for you?"

"You already know that one, Governor." He chuckled and gave her shoulders a gentle squeeze.

"Okay folks, now you're up to speed. Once I face the music with Chella I'll be returning to the Raptor."

"We'll be returning to the Raptor," said Nellie.

"Nellie, you guys ..."

"We made our choice, same as you, Dee. We're Red Nova now."

Deann nodded then reached for the comm unit at her shoulder. "Bridge."

"Bridge here."

"This is Deann, get me ship-to-ship, the Raptor."

"Raptor, aye. Just a minute. ... Go ahead Captain Deann."

"Raptor, this is Deann."

"Raptor here, Dornal commanding."

"Michella is sleeping. The Patriarch of Blue Nova has arrived, and I'm beat. I have to stay here until tomorrow."

"Understood."

Deann's voice softened. "Dor, tuck the kids in for me."

"I will."

"Dor, I'll be back tomorrow, I promise."

"I'll save up some energy." There was merriment in his voice and everyone relaxed.

"You'd better," grinned Deann, "you'll need it. Deann out."

"He's a good man, Ellie," said Deann as she saw the young witch looking at her, an expression of sadness on her elfin features. Ellie nodded and looked away.

Nellie's voice sounded in Deann's mind. "It's all right, Dee. Ellie knows how you feel."

"So, what's the plan?" asked Tarah. "All this mushy stuff is fine, but let's get to the point."

Deann stiffened. It had been a long time since anyone had spoken to her in that tone. Old Rath watched as she caught herself and ignored the sudden flash of resentment. "The plan is this; first, warn the king of the plot against him by Sega Clan."

"Already done," said Hawk.

"Step two: confer with the king and plan from there. He'll come to us, there's no one else he can trust at this point. Also, I'll give Chella back her ship. I command the Red Fleet. The captain of the Warbird will have to decide for herself what to do next. If she wants to sit back Hawk is welcome aboard the Raptor.

"Once we hit Arcalian space, we'll try to contact Micha and bring him up to speed. What he decides to do from there will determine where you folks fit in. Once we have the plot against King Borad under control, I plan to meet with Micha to see where Red Nova will fit in, or if we can't we'll have to find a home of our own."

Old Rath reached over to pat her hand. "Don't look too far ahead, Dee. Focus on what's at hand."

"I remember," she said, smiling. "I remember. All right, folks. I'm beat. I've fought a battle, escaped a trap in time, defeated the Iron Emperor, and commandeered a ship. It's been a full day and I'm tired. Everybody get some rest."

She rose and headed to the captain's quarters. Inside she stopped and looked all around. What was once so familiar, home, was strange to her now. She stripped off, showered, then fell onto the bed and slept. Seven hours later she arose, dressed in a fresh jumpsuit, the first she'd had in many years, and headed for the bridge.

Young Bim slid out of the captain's chair as she entered. "Captain on the bridge."

"Thanks, Bim. Report."

"All's quiet, Captain. Still heading towards Arcalian space, speed steady, your fleet is still behind us."

"Good to know. Get some rest now. I got this." He thanked her and left the bridge. The day crew began to arrive shortly. Once they were settled in she spoke. "Hawk, any news?"

"The king and his personal guard are headed for his hunting lodge at the edge of the Gap. He's asked us to meet him there."

"Done. Tell him to watch his back. Trust no one as I don't know who will strike at him." Hawk nodded and moved from weapons to comms. Ellie went to weapons. Once Hawk relaxed in his chair Deann spoke again. "Hawk, if Chella decides to take a different path you and your family will be welcome aboard the Raptor. All you have to do is ask."

"Thanks Dee, I'll keep that in mind."

Just then the comms came alive. "Sick Bay to Deann."

"'Lore, if you're going to beat me up can you do it off comms? This will be embarrassing for me."

"I should beat you up, but, Chella won't let me. She wants to see you, Dee."

"On my way. Hawk, take the chair." He moved easily to the captain's chair as she disappeared through the door.

Deann stepped through the door of the infirmary to see Michella sitting up, the baby asleep in a sling across her chest. Alore and Leen made a hasty exit, leaving the two lovers on their own to sort out their situation. Tears ran down Deann's face as she stepped closer and hugged Michella tightly. The baby squirmed in protest and kicked at her.

Smiling through her tears Deann pulled back to look at the child. "So, your Nova marks did stay blue. Well then, as matriarch of Red Nova, I greet you, Patriarch of Blue Nova."

"Dee, what are you talking about?"

"You were right all along, Chella. This little guy is special and beautiful. He'll become the father of a Nova Clan of his own, Blue Nova. Don't try to make a warrior out of him, Chella, that's not what he's meant to be."

"Dee?"

Deann hugged her tightly again. "Gods I love you, Michella. I've missed you so badly it's torn the heart out of me for years."

"Oh gods, Deann, you're leaving me, aren't you?"

"Lover, to you I was gone two weeks. For me it was nearly seven years. Seven years of hard battles and struggles to survive as well as keep my clan alive. Chella, they were a broken, hopeless people when I found them. They made me their chieftain and for years I've fought to keep them alive and get them out of that damned time ship."

"You broke our bond, chose a new lover, bore children, didn't you?"

"I had no other choice, Chella. None. I know you're hurting right now, so am I. I love you madly, always have, always will."

"But you're still leaving, going back to him."

"Them, Chella, I'm going back to them. Dor's a good man and he loves me. I'm extremely fond of him but my heart will always be yours. Sweetie, I can't stay. I'll leave Nellie here for you for a few days. Talk to her. Talk to Poppa Rath, too. I'll be on the Raptor as the chieftain should be." She hugged Michella again then released her. Brushing away her tears Deann spoke to the baby. "You be good to your mamma, mister, and I'll do everything in my power to see that you get the chance to become who you were meant to be." She turned and fled the infirmary.

Outside Alore was blocking her path. Deann hugged her tightly. "'Lore, you're the best friend I ever had and you always will be. I know that right now I'm the villain, and you're angry with me. I hope we can be friends again someday. Watch out for Chella for me."

"When we get to wherever we're going you've got some explaining to do."

"I will, I promise."

"Dee, take care of yourself."

Deann kissed her cheek and headed for the docking bay, reaching for her comms. "Bridge."

"Bridge here," replied Hawk.

"Contact the Raptor. Slow speed and lock up with her. I'm going home."

"Understood."

"Barah, Leen, Eddan, to the docking bay. Nellie, I need you to stay with Chella for a few days."

"Acknowledged," came the replies. "I'll talk to her, Dee," came Nellie's voice in her mind. "Just don't leave me behind."

"Wouldn't dream of it, Nellie. I can't lose the high priestess of Red Nova, now can I?"

The two ships locked up and the air locks opened. Before Deann could step in, a hand grabbed her arm and turned her around. She fought the instinct to fight. She turned and Michella stood facing her. Michella gazed into her eyes for a moment, then she relented. "Chieftain of Red Nova, permission to join your fleet."

"Chella?"

"I have no idea what the nine hells is going on, Dee, but I do know you. Permission to join the fleet."

"Granted, with thanks, Captain Michella. Have your pilot lay in a course for the Arcalian king's hunting lodge and transmit to the Raptor, then move the Warbird back between the Raptor and the Dragon for protection."

"Aye, aye, Chieftain," replied Michella. "When time permits will you talk to me?"

"Promise. Soon as time permits." Deann kissed Michella's cheek then turned and crossed to the Raptor.

Deann reached the bridge to find Tanie at the pilot station. "New course just transmitted and laid in, Chieftain."

"Pass it along to the Dragon and the Comet."

"Transmitted, Chieftain."

"Very good. Comms, fleet-wide including the Warbird."

"Comms, fleet-wide, ready Chieftain."

"Attention all ships, the Warbird will be joining us on our way to the hunting lodge of King Borad. Warbird, move into position." On her screen the ships moved to put the Warbird in the middle of the fleet. "People, we have a very important passenger aboard the Warbird. The Patriarch of Blue Nova has arrived. We'll escort him to the hunting lodge where it's my hope he can be introduced to his people. Helm, ahead three quarter speed."

"Three quarter speed, aye."

As the big ships leaped away the girl on comms turned to Deann. "Matriarch, the captain of the Warbird is calling, secure channel."

"Route it to my quarters. Dor, you have the bridge."

Deann walked heavily back to the captain's cabin. She smiled as she entered. This one felt like home. She sat on the edge of her bed and sighed. "Go ahead, Chella."

"You seem to know this man in my arms right now, Dee. Who is he?"

"Chella, these people I lead are my descendants of about a hundred generations or more. The Iron Emperor got his hands on an intergalactic time ship. He reappeared in their time and wiped out sector nine and all the Novans, tens of thousands of them. By then they'd formed three sub clans, Gold Nova who guarded the temple on Vakay, Blue Nova who were all the artists, singers, dancers, etc."

"And your Red Novans?"

"Defended everybody. That little guy is/was named Michan. He'll be the first Blue Novan."

Michella's voice was soft with wonder. "Because his marks stayed blue, didn't they."

"I'm guessing yes, but I have no way to know for sure. Chella, all I've got to work with is the history of my people as preserved by Eddan, an historian. There are a lot of gaps in it. I'm sort of making this up as I go along."

"That's my Deann, deal with what's in front of you and work on the rest later. So, are you planning to steal the rest of my crew?"

"Chel, I ..."

"Easy girl, easy. I'm just teasing. You've had seven years to wrap your head around this, I've only had a day and I've been a bit busy. Dee, can we talk more later?"

"Always."

"Dee, I love you madly, you know that."

"Yes, my heart, I know. I love you, too, more than anything."

"But I have to let you go. My father would say the needs of the clan are more important than my needs right now. As a captain, I have to accept that and work with it. You lead, Dee. For now, the Warbird is just another one of your ships. Michella out."

Deann sat staring at the floor for a long time before she returned to the bridge.

King and Clan

The trip was quiet for the next three days. Deann and Michella talked each day on a secure line. Slowly they were starting to get past the heartbreak. It was the fourth day when the klaxons sounded throughout the fleet and the command went out. "Battle stations. Battle stations. Chieftain to the bridge!"

Deann had been in the nursery playing with the children when the call came. She came pounding onto the bridge and threw herself into the captain's chair. "Report."

"Eight ships approaching, Chieftain. They're powering up weapons. They're hailing us."

"Gunners, target the lead ship. Fire on my mark only. Comms, let's hear from them."

"Attention approaching ships, you are in Nova Clan territory. Power down and prepare to be boarded. We'll relieve you of your cargo then let you be on your way."

"This is the Raptor, Deann of Red Nova commanding. You have ten seconds to make peace with your maker or to get the hell out of my way. Clock's ticking."

"Red Nova, never heard of ..."

Michella's voice cut in. "Zemma, it's Michella on the Warbird, move aside quick or she'll kill you all." That was all it took. The ships scattered like chaff in the wind.

Deann's image came up on Zemma's screen. "Zemma, it's Deann, remember me?"

"One-eyed Deann, the Giant Killer," replied Zemma. "I remember. Where'd you get the pretty ships?"

"Long story. I'll tell you some time. Right now I need a favor."

"Oh?"

"I need this route through the Gap plugged for a while, nothing goes in, nothing comes out. Can you do it?"

"Nothing nasty is going to come out of there, is it?"

"Probably not, but there's a slim chance. If it does it'll be a match for your ship, so don't play around, just kill it. If it isn't a Novan ship, kill it."

"Ah, there's not a lot of profit in a quick kill, if you know what I mean."

"Zemma, the things that could come through would have you in a slave collar so fast it would scare you."

The woman's voice hardened. "Right, a quick kill, no mercy and no prisoners."

"Thanks, I'll owe you one. Deann out."

The fleet hadn't even slowed down. They shot past the pirate ships and off into space. The pirates remained behind, Zemma's mind working furiously. She'd already planned to be working this area anyway and having the Giant Killer owe you a favor couldn't be a bad thing. Her curiosity was up, but the threat of a return to slavery was enough to stay her hand.

"Warbird calling, Chieftain."

"On screen."

"Dee, what was that about?"

"Chella, we're not one hundred per cent certain we destroyed all the enemy. Some of them might have made it to ships and some may have already been in ships when we blew the air locks on that monster. If anything followed us out they'll be looking for slaves to conquer. Zemma can watch our backs and it'll keep her out of my way until this is over."

"You know she'll want to collect on that favor."

"I know. I'll bring her a present if it all works out."

"A present. I have no idea what you're up to. Do your thing, crazy woman. Warbird out."

Deann settled back in her chair. "Eddan, you there?"

"On sensors, Chieftain."

"You did say that in the histories I joined up with pirates."

"Yes. Zemma was the name of the pirate leader according to the histories."

"I think this time I'll settle for an alliance," mused Deann.

Four days later they were nearing the planet where the king had his hunting lodge. This time they encountered a lone ship. Deann was on the bridge when the klaxon sounded the call to battle stations. The lone ship turned to face them. "Approaching ships, you're trespassing on Nova Clan territory, power down and identify."

Deann grinned as she heard that familiar voice. "This is the Raptor, Deann of Red Nova commanding. You fire at me, Zartah and you'll have a more exciting day than you bargained for."

"Deann? Where did you get all the ships?"

"Long story, and I'll be happy to tell it once everybody's on the ground and the king is safely here. I assume you were contacted by Hawk."

"We were. Is that the Warbird tucked in with all those pretty ships?"

"I'm here, Uncle Zartah," said Michella.

"What's going on? The king is in danger? He's coming here?"

"I'll explain all once everybody is on the ground," said Deann. "Is Micha near?"

"He'a about another day out. Deann ..."

"Put the Shield in beside the Warbird, Zartah. We'll move on together and wait in the air for Micha."

"Fine, don't tell me a damn thing, just drive me crazy. I presume those pretty ships are better than what we're flying."

"Yes they are and they're fully equipped with inertial dampeners too. Don't worry, Zartah, you'll be quite safe with us to protect you."

"Oh, thank the gods," he replied, as the Shield began to slowly move in beside the Warbird. "I'm so relieved." Deann's laughter could be heard throughout the fleet. Deann dropped the Raptor back and locked up with the Warbird. She retrieved her priestess and Hawk, then unhooked and led the fleet on their way. The next day they arrived in orbit above the hunting lodge. Hawk was instantly on the comms, but they were expected. The king was still three days out. Micha arrived in one.

"Ship inbound," said Hawk. He was at the sensors.

"Probably Micha," said Deann. "Let's have some fun with him. Comms, hail that ship."

"Hailing, aye. No response."

"He's trying to figure out why so many ships," grinned Hawk.

"Give me visual. Attention inbound ship," said Deann. "You are trespassing on Nova territory. Identify or be destroyed."

"This is the Ravage, Micha commanding, and I know damn well where I am. Deann, explain yourself."

"This is the Raptor, Deann of Red Nova commanding. Power down and prepare to be boarded."

"Deann, what are you up to? Where did you get those ships?"

"It's a long story, Micha. I'll be happy to tell it. Permission to come aboard?"

"Granted. I'll meet you in the conference room."

"Understood. Slow your rotation and we'll lock up with you." She signaled for the comms to be cut then spoke again. "Dor, the ship is yours. I shouldn't be more than a couple of hours. Comms, ship-to-ship."

"Ship-to-ship, aye."

"Warbird, Shield, I'm locking up with the Ravage. Put whoever you want into small fighters and join us. I'll try to get everybody up to speed."

As the Raptor moved into position to lock up with the Ravage, two heavily loaded fighters approached the Ravage and slipped inside. The two bigger ships locked up and the airlocks hissed open. Hawk, Pally, Eddan, and Nellie followed Deann onto the ship and headed for the mess hall. The room was nearly full. Everyone had gathered to hear

Deann's story. Nellie fairly flew into her mother's arms, tears of joy on her cheeks.

Micha was relaxed back in his chair. He kicked another over towards Deann, smiling. "Deann, report."

Deann batted aside the chair, her eyes hard as stone. "This isn't a social call. You need to pay attention, all of you."

Micha bristled at that as did the rest of Nova crew, but Nellie flicked her fingers, retrieving the chair and setting it down for Deann. "Easy, Dee. These folks are family, too. Go easy."

"Hold on," said Norlene, as she stepped up to Eddan. "I've seen those marks before." She turned to Deann and moved her tunic to see her tattoos. "Red Nova, now I remember. Micha, mind your manners now. We don't want this to get out of hand."

Deann forced her shoulders to relax. "Forgive me, Lady Norlene, Micha. I can be a bit hard-headed at times."

"I never would have guessed," replied Micha. He was grinning and Deann had to smile. She took the offered chair and sat facing him.

"Please people, I need you to pay close attention. Last time I saw most of you was about a month ago your time."

"Our time?" Arlessa asked softly. "Deann, how long has it been for you?"

"About seven years, give or take a bit. Please people, listen carefully to this man. Mark his words. Eddan, stay on topic now. Tell them about Red Nova and what happened to them, how we met and what happened from there to here."

Eddan took up the tale. He spoke of the numbers of Red Nova and Gold Nova. His voice shook as he spoke of the Iron Emperor's arrival and the decimation of sector nine. He paused for a moment then went on with the tale of Nova's destruction. He described the eventual defeat of the emperor by the remnants of Red Nova and of the years as refugees inside the time ship.

His voice gained a new warmth and power as he spoke of the arrival of the Matriarch and how she trained them for seven years before leading them against the emperor and their escape from the time ship.

When he finished they were all silent, trying to absorb some of what he'd said. Micha turned to Deann. "So you're the matriarch, the first Red Novan. You've led these people for seven years and brought them out of the time ship. I apologize for my tone earlier, fellow chieftain. What you've managed is no small feat. You've born them children?"

"We all have, Nellie's obviously carrying her second, I have two and Alise has three. We'll show them off once we're all on the ground with time for a visit." She turned to Michella. "I swear to you, we didn't expect to get back to our own time." She turned back to Micha.

Ena was leaning over his shoulder. "There's more, Micha, lots more."

Deann smiled. "Yes Ena, there's lots more. Eddan, tell them about the death of Borad, the first fall of Arcalia and the results of that."

Micha was paying close attention now. Borad was a friend, as well as the source of all the major supplies and ships he could want. Eddan finished speaking and Deann gave them all a moment to let that sink in. "All right, Eddan, show them the rest."

Eddan started the vid playing. "The second fall of Arcalia Prime as experienced by Red Nova. I was there as were several of the others."

"This is fact?" asked Arlessa, her voice cold.

"It was," replied Eddan.

"What's the significance?" asked Micha. "That's a long way in the future, right? Why show it to us now?"

"The reason that happened is because King Borad fell to Sega Clan," replied Deann. "Sega never did manage to get a firm grip, they were too stretched out trying to hold too much territory. That's why Arcalia fell, she had little or no defense. I plan to keep the king alive and thwart Sega's plans to seize Arcalian space.

"There are two reasons for that. First, by keeping Arcalia strong we retain a supply of ships and equipment. Second, that will keep Red Nova strong, far stronger than she was when the emperor struck. This time Red Nova will be waiting for him. If he comes in our timeline he'll come to his doom."

"This timeline will be very different, Deann," said Norlene. "You've already changed a number of things."

"Yes, and I'll change more." She reached for the comm at her shoulder. "Deann to Raptor."

"Raptor here, Dornal commanding."

"Dor, would you unhook the Raptor and go deliver that package for me. Make certain it reaches its destination."

"On my way, Chieftain. Dornal out."

Arlessa quirked an eye at Deann. "What was that about?"

"There was only one way off that damned time ship so we went for it. We attacked the bridge and fought our way in. When the emperor joined the battle we took him down, forced him to guide us out and blow the airlocks, then froze him solid."

"Oh gods, you've got my father on your ship," said Brenna.

"No ma'am, I have a robot on my ship, a very dangerous robot, but not for long," replied Deann. "Dor is on his way to dump the Iron Emperor into the sun. He'll shoot the crate containing the robot right at the star then watch to make certain it gets there. The Iron Emperor isn't coming back from this one."

"That's what I should have done," sighed Micha. "So, is that all of it?"

"Pretty much," replied Deann.

"And the plan is to warn Borad?"

"Already done, long since," said Hawk.

"Hawk, Poppa Rath, you guys are on board with this?" asked Micha.

"Better safe than sorry," replied Hawk.

"Gorda?"

"I'm with Hawk."

"Yeah, me too," said Micha. "All right, Chieftain Deann, this is your operation. Put us to work, What do you want us to do?"

Deann nodded, then took charge. Command had become second nature to her. "According to Hawk we have a couple of days to wait. I'd go out to meet him, but that might make him nervous and we're running low on food supplies. Put a fighter with good scanners in the air and I will too. The rest of us can find a spot to settle down and turn the hunters loose. That'll also give our people time to have a reunion, meet the folks of Red Nova, and get acquainted. It'll also give us time to talk."

"What's on your mind, Dee?"

"Once we put this to rest Red Nova will need a home, a place to be, a reason to be."

Arlessa stepped closer and took Deann by the shoulders. "According to your historian Red Nova had a home and a reason to be. I don't think we should change that, do you? Do any of you?"

"I sure don't," replied Norlene. "I've seen these people in action before."

"Where? When?" asked Arlessa.

"You know that I did a lot of time jumping when I was younger. I didn't recognize the Gap for what it was then, but I landed on a planet being invaded. Red Nova appeared and all hell broke loose. I managed to remain hidden, but I saw them, what they're capable of. Arlessa, you enhanced our crew, but these folk are their descendants. They're stronger, faster, and Deann has trained them like assassins.

"If these folk want to take on the job of protecting Nova Clan, I'm all for it."

Just then Deann's comm unit squawked. "Raptor to Chieftain Deann."

"Go ahead."

"Package delivered, Chieftain. Delivery confirmed."

"Understood. Dor, put up a fighter to keep an eye out for the king or intruders then take the fleet down. You and Alise need to go hunting. I want meat and I'm getting hungry."

"Oh yes, Matriarch, it will be my undying pleasure to provide meat for you. Dornal out."

"That's him, isn't it?" asked Edie.

"The father of my children, yes. I know you're angry with me ..."

"I would never have abandoned Micha."

"I'm not as strong as you and Brenna, Edie. I'm just trying to work it out as I go along," Deann replied gently.

"Easy, lover," said Micha. "It was different for Deann. She had a clan to nurture. From the moment she accepted the title of chieftain it wasn't about her or Chella any longer. It was about the clan. You'd have done the same, any of us would."

He reached for the comm unit on his shoulder. "Bridge."

"Bridge here."

"Launch a fighter to keep watch, then set her down with the fleet."

"Aye, chieftain. Launching fighter."

Alliance

As the Ravage settled to the ground and the hatch opened they found Alise and Dor waiting for them. "Orders, Matriarch?" she asked, merriment clear in her voice. Deann grinned in return.

"Alise, hand that child over to its grandmother then organize a hunting party, you have a fleet to feed."

"Understood. Dor, Korim hunters, Miriam, to me, quickly." She turned, and with a shy smile, passed the bundle in her arms to Keira. "This is Little Keira. Watch her, she bites." Alise glanced over her shoulder as she led her hunters into the forest. She smiled as she saw Keira showing the baby to Rathbone. She turned to focus on the hunt.

Leen suddenly appeared beside Deann. She began to chatter away, reminding Deann of her promise to speak to the clan about the Eldin. "Looks like you have work to do, Chieftain," grinned Micha. "Better get to it."

"Understood," chuckled Deann. "All right, Leen. Bring the Eldin. Nellie."

Deann whispered to Nellie who nodded then shimmered her ragged jumpsuit into the flowing scarlet robes she used for official business. She stepped forward and her voice carried across the wide clearing to all present. "Red Nova, assemble." Nova Clan was astounded at the speed with which the ships emptied and Deann's clan gathered before her.

Nellie gave them a moment to gather then she spoke again. "Red Nova, we gather to hear the petition of the Eldin. Leen, you may speak."

Leen gave a little squeak as Pally tossed her in the air, but she settled on his shoulders easily. She gazed imploringly at the assembled clan.

"People of Red Nova, fellow clansfolk. I was born of the Eldin, yet you accepted me, nurtured me, and accepted me into the clan. I now ask you to do the same for these seven people of the Eldin race. They're lost and far from home. They cannot get back. Please Red Nova, they're great healers and I know they'll be good for the clan. Will you accept them?"

"Who will speak for these folk?" asked Nellie.

"I speak for them," replied Leen.

"What say you, Red Nova?" asked Nellie.

"Keep them," called Quint. "I need a healer on my ship."

"As do I," said Girta. "Keep them I say."

There were a few more calls of "Keep them."

"What say you, Matriarch?" asked Nellie.

"I say we keep them," said Deann. "Welcome to Red Nova, people." There was a rousing cheer then Nellie called for silence again. When the folk settled down Deann spoke again. "I now appoint Leen chief medical officer for Red Nova. Leen, assign your people, at least two to a ship."

Leen squealed with delight as she hopped off Pally's shoulders and began to chatter away to the other Eldin.

The meeting was breaking up and the people were starting to prepare fire pits when Miriam came pounding out of the trees. She went straight to Micha and Deann. "Men in the trees, many dozens, coming this way. They're armed and trying to move quietly. The others remained to watch them."

"All yours, Dee," grinned Micha.

"Miraim, bring the hunters back. Nellie, sound battle stations. Micha, take your people to the right, enhanced warriors to the fore, humans behind with long range weapons, small children, nursing mothers, and elders in the Shield. Get that ship in the air."

"Quint, Girta, all fighters into the trees, there. Leen, children, healers, nursing mothers, elders in the Comet. Eddan, get the Comet off the ground, now."

Nellie's robes had shimmered to black and there was witch fire dancing all around her. As soon as she'd called for battle stations she stepped to Deann's right hand and faced the forest. Deann was startled to see Ellie step to her left and the two elder witches to the right and left of the younger. "Command us now, Deann," said Arlessa. "What do you need?"

"We're the bait," replied Deann. "If they come at us hard we back away and lure them into the kill zone."

"Do we have to kill them, Dee?" asked Ellie. She bristled at the tone of Deann's reply.

"We do. If you can't, then get back into the woods with Micha's crew." Ellie glared at her, but then the hunters came pouring out of the trees. "Hunters, to me." They came. "Defend the witches."

"Deann, we need no ..."

"It's all right, Mamma, we'll just step back and let Red Nova show us how it's done," said Ellie. She stepped back to allow Alise to take her place. The others did too, including Nellie.

"How long, Alise."

"Any moment now."

"Nellie, if you spot a leader, hang him up for me. I'd like a few questions answered."

"Understood, Chieftain."

Suddenly a mass of armed men erupted from the forest. Micha recognized Sega Clan colors. Deann opened fire as did her companions. They started to back away. The oncoming men were firing as they charged into the clearing, but the leader sensed a trap. He tried to hold his men back, but it was too late. Deann screamed her battle cry and charged right at the superior force.

Nellie, Dor, and Alise were right at her side, but the move took the others by surprise and they were a step behind. At Deann's cry Red Nova burst out of the trees and attacked the enemy force. Nova Clan waded in from the opposite side, but it was Red Nova who demolished the attackers. Outnumbered by ten-to-one or more made no difference. Micha was stunned at their speed and prowess as they fought.

The battle was bloody and swiftly over. Hundreds of fighting men charged from the trees and barely two dozen survived to flee into the forest. "Hunt them," bawled Deann. "Run them down. Let none escape." Like hounds on the trail, the warriors of Red Nova raced into the trees. "Nellie?"

"Lady Arlessa has three for you to question," replied Nellie, "and Ellie has two more."

Deann nodded then grabbed her comm unit. "Deann to Leen."

"Leen here, Matriarch."

"Fun's over. Get your healers out here now. Gold Nova is beating you to it."

"Understood." Leen and the other Eldin came running out of the Comet, which had just landed, swiftly spreading out over the battlefield. They could hear her shouting orders in Eldin.

"Leen, Novans first. Novans only for now." The woman waved her arm that she understood, then bent to her task.

Deann spun with a speed that startled everybody. She stepped up to the first man Arlessa held in place. "Who are you?"

"Up your's, scut ..." He fell with a dagger in his chest. She stepped to the next one. "Who are you?"

The man swallowed hard and, with wide eyes, replied. "Orfat of Sega."

"Who commanded your party?"

The man nodded to the dead man at her feet. "He did."

"Who was he?"

"Kiron of Sega, first cousin to Kemge of Sega, clan chieftain."

"Why were you here? What was your mission?" He swallowed hard, but didn't speak. "Nellie, see if you can loosen this one's tongue a bit."

Nellie started to take a step forward, but he began to weep. "No, please. We were sent here to kill Micha. It's well known he uses this planet to resupply."

Micha's voice sounded right behind Deann. "I warned Kemge what would happen if he came at me again. Looks like I need to take a trip."

"There's more, Deann," said Ena.

"Tell me the rest," demanded Deann. "Speak or I'll have Nellie roast you alive."

"The king," he stammered. "The king of Arcalia comes here. We were supposed to kill him if he arrived, but our mission was primarily to kill Micha and put his daughters in chains."

"Put these men in restraints," said Deann, as she turned away. "We'll give them to the king. That is, unless you want them, Micha. After all it was you they were here for."

Micha just grinned at her. "What would you do in my place?"

"Kill them." Everyone fell silent and stared at her. "Never leave a live enemy behind you. If the assassins sent keep vanishing soon no more will come. Once warned, you know they're coming. If you send them back to Kemge with a warning, he'll be watching for you."

"It's a hard line to walk, isn't it, Dee," Micha said kindly, "being chieftain of a small hunted people without losing your soul in the process."

"Yeah, it is." She sighed. "So, we give them to the king? He can hold them long enough for us to get to Kemge."

"Us to get to Kemge?" asked Micha.

"I have an issue here as well."

"Deann, let me deal with Kemge. You focus on your original plan." She thought for a moment then nodded. "Dee, I have to admit, I sure wouldn't want to go up against that clan of yours."

She smiled her pride in her clan. Leen approached, a bright smile on her face. "Report," said Deann.

"We had a few injuries, two bad, but they will recover in a few days, and we have nineteen injured enemies. What should I do with them? No, don't say it because you know I won't do it. I can't do that. Chieftain, I ..."

Deann took her by the shoulders and smiled. "Patch them up, Leen. We'll give them to the king. He can decided what to do with them."

Relief washed over the Eldin's face. She suddenly hugged Deann then sprinted away, calling to the other healers. Arlessa, Edie, and Alore were already working with the prisoners. "Where did you ever find them?" asked Micha.

"On the time ship. They were Loran's slave healers. They're a special people, my Eldin."

"She keeps you human?"

"Like no other can," replied Deann. "I know keeping those men alive could be a bad mistake, but ..."

"There has to be places a chieftain won't go," said Micha. "Deann, I'm disappointed as all hell about what's hurting Chella, but I have to admit. I'm mighty proud of you as well."

"Thank you, Micha, that means a lot, but it's still not going to work."

"What are you talking about?"

"You're not retiring and making me grand chieftain. I'm already in over my head with Red Nova. So just forget it."

"Why, Deann, that thought never ..."

"You're a terrible liar, too. It's your eyes, Pappa Micha. They give you away every time."

"You'd be good, Dee. I could go back to farming with a clear conscience."

"Not going to happen. Look, there come the hunters."

Rathbone was approaching them with Keira at his side. They were herding three men ahead of them. "Micha, we managed to catch three for you to question. Deann's savages finished the rest. I doubt any survived."

"Oh?"

"No, they didn't kill any prisoners," said Rathbone. "They're just so damned fast and deadly. Their opponents don't survive long enough to surrender."

"I'm Micha," he said, as he stepped in front of the captives. "You failed." They didn't answer.

"Where's your ships?" asked Deann. Still no answer. She moved, there was the sound of her blow landing and a man fell. She turned to the next man. "Where's your ships?"

"Gone," he replied, not meeting her eyes. "We've been stuck on this godforsaken insect nest for months, just waiting."

"Where's your camp?"

"Two hours, that way."

"Anybody left there?" she asked.

"No, when we saw the ships landing we knew the target was in play. All hands moved out."

"How many of you were there?"

"Two hundred forty-four elite troops."

"Those weren't elite troops," said Rathbone. "Today you faced real elite troops. What do we do with them, boss?"

"Put them with the rest of the prisoners. We'll sort this out later. Rath, post some of our folk to guard them. Red Nova earned their rest today." Rathbone nodded and moved his captives over to join the rest. "Maybe we should save the hunting for another day."

"Not a chance," said Deann. "Look." Micha looked to see the original hunting party entering the forest again.

"They're leaving us to clean up the battlefield," grinned Micha.

"So it seems." Deann reached for her comms. "Deann to Quint."

"Quint here, Chieftain."

"Organized a party to stack the dead against the trees then move the camp down beside the river. Get a few fires going. The hunters should be back soon. Girta."

"Here, Chieftain."

"Send up a fighter to keep an eye out down here. I don't want any more surprises."

"Understood."

Deann could hear Micha giving orders for his crews to help Red Nova with the clean up and moving the camp down closer to the river. By the time darkness fell the camp had been moved, ships moved closer, and the hunters had returned with three large beasts they had killed. Meat was soon roasting over the fires.

Deann was still fussing over her clan. She spoke to each and every one, made sure the children were all right, the elders cared for, etc. When the meat was declared ready, the women and children came forward to eat. Nova Crew stood back watching as Red Nova waited for the young women and children to get their food then the warriors lined up. Micha smiled as he watched his own people follow the example of Deann's clan.

"Not hungry, Dee?" asked Michella, as she approached with Nova Crew.

"Famished," replied Deann. "My turn soon."

"Do you always allow your clan to eat first?" asked Zartah.

"Always. First the children, nursing mothers, and the elders eat. Once they're fed then the warriors eat. Then it's my turn." Nellie and Barah had held back beside her, as had Dor, Pally, Alise and the two ship's captains.

"I grow more and more impressed each moment," said Arlessa. "Looks like it's our turn now."

The feasting went on well into the night. Stories were exchanged, new friendships began, and more. Arlessa looked on, smiling her delight. Nova was growing, prospering. King Borad had been right, the Nova she dreamed of wasn't a planet, it was a people. This people. Now came the task of fitting Red Nova into the mix. These were a fierce and savage clan, utterly devoted to Deann. Deann, in her turn was completely devoted to them and she had proved to be an able leader.

"Don't try to rush it, Lessa," said Norlene, as she leaned over to whisper to Arlessa. "I know what you're thinking, and I agree, just let it evolve. They'll stay with us, become true Novans."

"You know, Norlene, I think they're the true Novans, the fruits of our efforts, the results of our dreams."

"Yes, they're what our people will someday become."

Deann finally gave it up and sought out her bed. Dor grunted and rolled over to take her in his arms. "About time you called it a day, girl." He kissed her forehead and cuddled her close.

Deann sighed deeply as she allowed the fatigue to claim her. "Dor, are you ever going to tell me?" she murmured.

"Tell you what, sweetheart?"

"You've had a secret as long as we've been together. Lately it's been on your mind. Tell me what's going on."

"Nothing for you to worry about. Go to sleep now."

"Dor, don't make me beat it out of you. I held back from Chella for months and finally spoke to her. Everything could have been solved if I had just spoken up. Dor, I will never leave you and I don't want anything to come between us. Talk to me, please."

"All right, Chieftain nosy britches. It's something from the histories, and I can tell by the way you're acting that Eddan hasn't told you about it."

"Told me what? Dor, what's he holding back. I need to know."

"Probably just slipped his mind, or he doesn't think it's his business to say."

"So tell me. Tell me or I'll ..."

"The matriarch had two companions."

It took a few moments for Deann's tired brain to absorb what he had just said. "Dor, are you saying I, the historical me, had two bonded companions?"

"Yes. Dee, I love you madly, but I've always expected I'd have to share your affections with another. You've mourned the loss of her as long as I've known you. I don't doubt your love for me, I don't, but I know full well you still love her too. She's hurting, Dee, and so are you. Talk to her. Sort this out, for both your sakes."

"Are you telling me you would accept a three-way bond?"

"Not my first choice, but I've had seven years to prepare myself. Look, Barah told me all about her when he was teaching me to fly a ship. He warned me you'd never forget her. I've always known your feelings and I accept that. I hope she and I can become friends."

"Friends."

"Yeah, well, she is pretty cute and ..."

With a shriek Deann leaped astride him and began to beat him with the pillow. Laughing, Dor protected himself as much as possible. Finally she stopped and kissed him deeply. When their lips parted she melted against him. "You're such a nut."

"Talk to her, Dee. You're both hurting and there's no need of it."

"Shut up and go to sleep."

"Yes, Chieftain." She poked him in the ribs again and he chuckled then cuddled her closer.

Deann was still pondering what he'd said as she drifted off to sleep.

Dawn arrived and Micha stepped out of his ship to find the entire clan of Red Nova outside exercising. First they did a series of stretches, then moved into combat training. He watched approvingly, as did Murtah, who had joined him. "What do you think, Murtah?"

"I think Deann's stolen my job as combat master," chuckled the big man. "Impressive, aren't they?"

"They sure were yesterday," said Micha. "I wouldn't want to go against them. Did you notice how Deann made certain we were back a bit and more protected."

"I did notice that. Ah, looks like they're finished and the cooks are getting busy. I suppose the warriors eat last again."

"I'd say that's a safe bet."

Micha grinned and walked over to join Deann who was overseeing the feeding process. She had a child at her breast and another clinging to her leg. As Micha approached Leen appeared and took the children now that the baby had been fed. Micha spoke softly to Murtah who stepped back a bit and reached for his comms. Nova Clan women and children began arriving to join in the morning meal. Nova's cooks got into the action and soon it was time for the warriors to eat.

Micha watched carefully. Several of the Red Nova warriors bolted their food then rose to board two small ships. They rose into the air and the two that had been in orbit returned. He saw the guards on the prisoners relieved and then the people on watch also relieved. They came and ate before seeking their bunks. Only then did Deann invite him to join her for a meal.

They sat among the warriors, enjoying their breakfast. Old Rath and Eddan were swapping tales, Rathbone and Quint were exchanging wrist hold techniques, and so it went. "Looks like everybody's getting along all right," said Deann.

"Seems like," agreed Micha. "You were concerned?"

"A bit, but I think we're all good ... except for me."

"You?"

"Yeah, me. I have some serious sucking up to do."

He laughed. "Oh yeah, that you do."

"I thought Edie was going to tear my head off. You seem to be handling things a bit better."

"I know why you did what you did, Deann. I know you had no choice; you still don't."

"Yeah, everybody thinks it's so great to be a clan chieftain."

"You could have refused the job."

"Sure, like you did. No, Pappa Micha, neither of us had a choice. Pappa Rath says you just have to deal with what's in front of you, like it or not. That's why he became governor of the Arlen Alliance. Too many people would have died if he hadn't. Same for you. Sector Nine would all be in slave chains if you'd said no to the job."

"And Red Nova would be no more without you, Deann. Look, we have some sorting out to do, but ..."

"Forget it, Micha. I will not take on chieftain of all Novans while you go build another sweet little farm somewhere on Vakay."

He gave a great bellowing laugh at that and hugged her shoulders. "Ah well, it was worth a shot."

"There's a fine thing, Father," said Alore, as she sat beside him, "cuddling up to the enemy while your daughter hides in her cabin."

"I'm not hiding in my cabin, Lore," said Michella as she joined them, sitting beside Deann, "and Dee's not our enemy, she's your best friend. Remember that."

"Yes, but, dammit, Chella, she cheated on you and you sit there ..." She suddenly burst into tears.

Deann reached across Micha to take Alore's hand in hers. "Lore, I didn't cheat. I broke that bond and my heart that day, but I did what I had to do to help these people survive. You'd do the same, you'd run the same risks for your people."

"But, how could you just ...?

"Listen you. My memory is still pretty good. Now you stop picking on me or I'll tell Krak-sul about that certain young man you've been eyeing up and he'll have a chat with ..."

"Oh my gods, don't you dare say a word to that overprotective ... Hey what did you just do, Deann of Red Nova?"

Deann grinned and released her hand. "I changed your state and blackmailed you at the same time."

"You're evil."

"'Lore, I'm worse than that some days. Micha, I think we've got trouble brewing.

Micha leaped to his feet. "Dammit, some days a man can't get a minute's peace. Chella, get your ship in the air."

Deann was already bawling orders as her small ships reached the ground. They followed the big ships into the air again then entered the launch bays. They reached orbit to see ten ships inbound on the sensors. The excitement was caused by the fifty ships chasing the ten. "Ravage to Raptor. That's king Borad in the ten ships. That's Sega Clan after him."

"Understood," replied Deann.

"Deann, you have the superior ships, you command the fleet."

"Acknowledged. Gold Nova go right, Red Nova go left. We'll let the king pass then we'll deal with Sega Clan. All hands to battle stations."

A few moments later the ships began to check in. "Dragon; battle ready and awaiting orders, Chieftain."

"Comet; standing by and battle ready, Chieftain."

"Warbird; ready, Raptor."

"Shield; ready."

"Ravage; ready and awaiting orders. Chieftain, do you want to deploy the witches in fighters. We're a bit outnumbered here."

"Hold the Ladies in reserve, Ravage. We shouldn't need them, but be ready just in case. Warbird."

"Warbird here."

"Have Hawk let the king know the plan. Tell the king to hold back and let Nova deal with this."

"He won't like it," came Hawk's voice.

"I don't care," replied Deann. "His safety is of the utmost importance. All right, fleet, ahead three quarter speed."

The ships leaped ahead and Micha started muttering. Deann's three quarter speed was closer to his full speed. They swiftly reached the fleeing king and his ten ships. Nova Clan split into two groups to let him pass. The Sega Clan ships began to hail the fleet. "Oncoming ships, identify in the name of the true king of Arcalia.

"This is the Raptor, Deann of Red Nova commanding. Reverse your course or die. You have ten seconds to comply." There was a sudden barrage of bluster and threats, but Deann signaled Tanie to cut the connection. "Fleet, attack speed. Ravage, we'll pull them around so you can get at them from behind."

Micha's reply was lost in the sudden madness of battle. Deann's predators leaped at the tight formation of oncoming ships. Suddenly they split apart and wove among the flank ships, firing as they sped through the formation. The Sega ships were slow and clumsy, and their weapons fire did more damage to their own fleet than to the lightning fast attackers. A dozen or more ships exploded or went limp in space as Red Nova made their pass through.

Once through the enemy formation Red Nova made an impossible tight banking turn and came back in. The entire enemy fleet was focused on them now. That's when Gold Nova hit them from behind. The enemy fleet had been reduced to half before they even began to launch their smaller fighters. The Novan ships rolled and spewed out fighter ships as well. Once again, the superior ships proved devastatingly effective. Within moments the enemy fighters were struggling to return to the mother ships.

And then it was over. The comms came alive. "Stop, stop, we surrender. Stop. We surrender."

"This is Deann of Red Nova. Be it known by one and all, Red Nova takes no prisoners. We never retreat, we never surrender, and we don't take prisoners. You've entered our territory with ill intent. You're not going home."

"Wait, wait, you can't just kill us all."

"Watch me."

"Wait, wait, what do you want?"

"I want King Board back on his throne. I want Kemge of Sega's head on a pike. I'll accept your surrender this one time only. Go back to that scheming coward and tell him, Red Nova will come for him and there'll be no place for him to hide, no force large enough to protect him. Go, before I change my mind." The surviving ships turned and fled back the way they had come.

"Raptor to Ravage."

"Ravage here."

"Did we leave anybody on the ground watching the prisoners?"

"You didn't," chuckled Micha, "but I did. I left a number of our human crewmen to guard them. The prisoners will still be there."

"Guess I blew that. Let's just wait around a bit until we're sure those characters truly have gone home."

"Oh, they went home all right," came another voice. "This is Borad of Arcalia. Just who are you, Deann of Red Nova, and why are you so intent to put me back on my throne. Don't mistake me, I'm grateful in the extreme, but ..."

"That's a long story, Sire," replied Deann. "I'd be delighted to share it on the ground. Can your hunting lodge accommodate all of us?"

"Easily. I'll lead the way."

"Excuse me, Sire, but we were on the ground and encountered a number of people who meant to do you harm. A few survived to become our prisoners. If I may, I'd like to send a few Novan into the lodge, just to be sure it's clear."

"As you wish, my savior. However, there are a dozen custodians in that lodge. I'd like them to survive."

"Tell them to step outside. Raptor to Warbird."

"Warbird here."

"Is Hawk familiar with the hunting lodge?"

"Intimately," came his voice.

"Good," said Deann. "All yours, Chella. Make sure we have a safe home to go to."

"Understood."

The Warbird dropped like a stone. She entered the atmosphere then spilled out her small fighters. With the big ship hovering overhead, the crews of the fighters spread throughout the enormous lodge then reported in that all was clear. The Warbird reported to the fleet, then the ships began to settle to the ground on the launch pads just outside the walled building.

The King

The Raptor and the Ravage hung in the sky while the other ships landed and organized themselves. The king's men found the prisoners and took charge of them, while the king was carefully ensconced in his royal quarters with his brother. When Deann was finally satisfied that the Sega Clan ships weren't going to return, the final two ships landed.

The hunters raced to the forest while the king's men showed the cooks where the great kitchens were located. A quick discussion between Gold Novan and Red Novan cooks decided they would rather work outside on the open. Fire pits were dug, fires built, the king's men brought huge spits for the roasting of game.

Hawk appeared and found Micha, Gorda, and Deann. He led them to the king's quarters. Deann insisted Eddan accompany her as well. Hawk agreed. The king sat quietly as he listened to Eddan's story then he watched, stony faced while the vid played out the final fall of Arcalia. "You swear this is truth?"

"I was there for the final fall, Sire, as were those few of my compatriots who survived the final battle."

The king showed no emotion at all, except a deep sadness. "How did it all come to this?"

"You were betrayed and killed, Sire," said Deann. "Sega Clan then used your successor as a puppet until they killed him and annexed Arcalia into Sega Clan territory. Sega was too spread out to make a serious defense."

"What is your stake in all this, young woman?"

"Red Nova was my legacy in that timeline, my descendants. They all perished, except these few I happened upon in the time ship. In

116

other words, your death inadvertently led to the destruction of my children. Sire, with you gone, Nova had no access to supplies, no ships. They turned to piracy for they had no other option. Without you, Arcalia is weak. Without you, Nova is weak.

"I want to put you back on your throne because I want Nova to be strong. I want Nova ready and waiting if that monster comes back in this timeline. This time it'll be a very different Arcalia and Nova that he'll face, if he comes. If not, then no harm dome at all."

"Micha?"

"Sire, I have to say, I'm with Deann here."

"Gorda?"

"Oddly enough, it all makes sense to me." Gorda grinned. "Besides, think how boring it would be to spend the rest of your life hiding in the Gap."

"Somehow I doubt it would be boring. Brother?"

"I trust Deann," said Hawk. "When we had that emergency with Michella's capture Deann showed her mettle. Time and again she's proven to be an exceptional leader as well as a fearsome warrior. I trust her and believe in her. I have no idea what she has in mind, but I'm anxious to hear it."

"So, Deann of Red Nova, the idea is to make Arcalia strong again?"

"It is, Sire. A strong Arcalia is the key to the ultimate success of Nova and the survival of Sector Nine. With Arcalia strong my people, my children, will thrive. That's my goal."

Borad smiled, he was getting past the numbness and shock of being deposed. "That is indeed a worthy goal, and one I personally am in favor of," he said. "Have you a plan to see this all happen?"

Deann sighed and relaxed deeper into her chair. "In truth, Sire, I've sort of been making it up as I go along." That brought a round of chuckles. "I do have a few ideas, though."

"I'd love to hear them."

Deann was suddenly shy. These were older and much wiser men, men she had always looked to for wisdom and succor as well as advise. Now they were all looking to her for answers. "Well, to start with, we have to get you back on the throne."

"You may have already done that, Dee," said Hawk. "You sent Sega packing with a warning that you would come for Kemge. Knowing that Nova survived his trap and is coming for him will cause him to withdraw into his stronghold. That'll leave our cousin, the conniving little usurper, shivering on his stolen throne. He'll have to run for it because the military won't support him while Borad's alive. If you escort Borad back to Arcalia Prime, the military will fall in behind you and Goro will run for his life."

"Straight to Sega Clan," muttered the king. "Ah well, it'll be the Viceroy's task to dig him out."

"If he'll get involved," said Hawk.

"He will," said Micha, "as soon as Eddan gives him a future history lesson he'll act."

The king sighed and relaxed at last. "And that puts me back on my throne, removes the plotter and traitors, and makes Arcalia stronger than ever, while removing the Sega Clan threat. Only one more thing remains to be understood. Young woman, what's this all going to cost me? You're not going to bankrupt my kingdom are you?"

Deann laughed at that. "No Sire, all I want is supplies and new ships."

"New ships? Girl, you're already flying better ships than anything else the galaxy has to offer, including the best Arcalia can produce. Micha already has our best and has added inertial dampeners to them. Your ships have the inertial dampeners as well, as I've seen this day. Why would you ask me for ships?"

Deann leaned her elbows on her knees and smiled at him with her most winning smile. "Sire, do you think your engineers would like to get a look at one of my ships?"

His eyes opened wide and he grinned. "Are you saying what I think you're saying?"

"Uh-huh. I'll stuff my whole clan into the two best I've got and give you the old Comet to use as you see fit. My ships are pretty beat up and they're old. I want new ships built on that design."

"Keep your ship, Deann," replied the king. "Just give my men a week to go over her then we'll build you better ships and give you as many as you want."

"A dozen would be nice. Six for me and six for Micha. Oh, and while we're here I'd like to have my people go over your personal ship."

"My ship? Why?"

"Sire, it's my crew who developed the inertial dampeners. You need a powerful witch to make the key chips, but it can be done. I'd like to install the dampeners on your personal ship. That way, if you ever need to make a run for it ..."

"I'll have a much better chance for survival. Deann, you've already saved my life this day, and now you're being extremely generous. Tell me what else you need."

"Well, Sire, we depleted our munitions and fuel today and my folks could use some new clothes. We've been on the run for a lot of years."

"No time to go shopping."

"Exactly."

"You'll have it, Deann, all of it. We can rob the ships that fled with me for fuel and munitions. That was a timely warning, by the way. Hawk's first message was quite cryptic, but timely."

"Oh?"

"I received a message. It said only one word. Run. I took every ship at the palace and headed for here as he knew I would. Enough of this. Let's go see if those hunters of yours have returned yet. I'm in the mood for venison."

While the preparations for a feast continued, the prisoners were brought before the king for questioning. Lady Arlessa used her magic truth powder on them and they told all, the plot to kill Micha and the King. Borad had them loaded into the brig of one of his ships. "Captain Xeran, take that lot and find the Viceroy. Give him this copy of the confession, give him Micha's message, then remain with his fleet until it is safe to return home."

"As you command, Sire." The man saluted and strode to his ship, bawling orders as he went. The ship soon lifted off and disappeared into the sky.

The next day, the king's men looted their own ships as well as the Lodge's stores to top up all the Novan ships with fuel and munitions. Pally and his crew of engineers installed the inertial dampeners on the King's personal ship then gave the ship's crew a quick rundown on how they worked and some of the hazards. The next morning all the ships rose and set course for Arcalia Prime. They had about two weeks travel at three quarter speed. There was time to relax a bit.

Eight days later a fleet consisting of half of the Arcalian military appeared in their path. The call to battle stations sounded and all ships were instantly ready. "King Borad to Raptor."

"Deann here, Sire."

"All right, my savior. Take command. Do we run or do we fight?"

"Let's find out who they are first. Maybe we can bluff our way out of this one. Raptor to Ravage."

"Ravage here. Orders Chieftain."

"There's a lot of them, Micha. If I can't bluff them out you may need to deploy your witch gunners."

"Understood. Ravage standing by."

"Tanie, hail them."

"They're hailing us, Chieftain."

"On screen."

"Approaching ships, you have entered Arcalian space. Identify."

"This is the Raptor, Deann of Red Nova commanding. Our fleet is escorting King Borad of Arcalia back to Arcalia Prime. Your turn, identify yourselves."

"A worthy effort, pirate. However, His Majesty has been assassinated. King Goro rules Arcalia now."

"The hell he does, Admiral," came Borad's voice. "Check your screen. As you can see I'm very much alive, but that damned usurper won't be for much longer."

"King Borad? Sire? Is that truly you? You're alive?"

"Yes, Daran old friend, I'm still very much alive thanks to Nova Clan, especially that young woman who just spoke to you. So, what now, old friend? Do we do battle or do we continue on together?"

"Sire, my fleet is yours to command, as ever."

"Excellent, contact Deann of Red Nova aboard the Raptor and place yourself under her command."

"Sire?"

"She and her merry band of savages are the reason I'm still alive, Daran. Trust me in this."

"As you command, Sire. This is the Excelsior calling the Raptor. Awaiting orders, ma'am."

"Admiral Daran, this is Deann of Red Nova. Form a proper escort for His Majesty and escort him back to Arcalia Prime. Nova will hide behind you, but will be ready in case we meet resistance. If we do meet resistance open a path to let us through. We'll deal with it."

"You'll deal with it?"

"You have your orders, Admiral. Raptor out. Raptor to Ravage."

"Ravage here." His grin could easily be heard in Micha's voice.

"Gold Nova on the king's right. Red Nova to the king's left. Lead on, Sire."

"Leading on, aye," came the king's chuckle.

Once again they set out. Messages went out ahead and more Arcalian military ships came to join the fleet. By the time they approached Arcalia Prime there was a wild celebration going on world wide. The usurper had fled, and King Borad was welcomed home by the entire population of the Arcalian kingdom and allied territories.

It was several days before the excitement settled down. After that, the king's engineers descended on the Comet. Pally stayed with them, explaining what worked and why. They took copious notes, measurements, and photos of key systems. They got more and more excited, then one day Pally and crew took them up for a run so they could observe the ship in operation.

Meanwhile, Ellie took Tanie on a wild shopping spree. Tanie was awestruck at Ellie's ability to locate and procure the more unusual items that would be useful in the Gap. Deann complained they would have to use the Comet for a transport scow if they didn't stop shopping.

The engineers played with the ship, the procurers shopped, and Hawk hunted. Over the eight days they were there, several highly placed people died suddenly of unnatural causes and three by outright bloodshed. A number of others tried to flee, but Admiral Daran's fleet ran them down. There was great concern in the court, as King Borad seemed to have lost his usual good humor. He was cleaning house and taking no prisoners.

On the ninth day the Viceroy and the High Priestess arrived. They were received at court, then quietly whisked away to a private meeting with the king and Nova Clan. Once again Eddan told the tale of the fall of Arcalia and Sector Nine. At the viewing of the vid the High Priestess lost her stomach contents. Pale and shaken she demanded to know why they had been shown this horror.

"What was the point of all this?" asked Marla, High Priestess.

"The point," said Deann, "is that Sega Clan is too aggressive. By not reining them in you allow the fall of Arcalia, the destruction of Sector Nine, and eventually all of Nova."

"You believe this to be truth?" asked Lortax, the viceroy.

"I was there," Eddan replied softly. "I can summon others who were there as well to speak to you. Much of what you've seen was captured from their personal recorders."

"Well, we could bring this to the Clan Council. You could post a formal complaint there."

Micha snorted. "Lortax, I swear to you, Kemge of Sega won't live long enough to reach that council meeting. He was warned what would happen if he came at me again." He reached for his comm unit. "Micha to Zartah."

"Here, boss."

"Mount up, we're going after Kemge."

"Understood."

"Micha, for the love of the gods, he'll have a thousand ships in the air to protect him."

"So did Loran," replied Micha, as he turned to go.

"Micha, want company?" asked Deann.

"No, you defend the Gap until I get back."

"Just make sure you come back."

"I always do."

At that point Lortax stepped forward. "Wait, Micha. Dammit all, just wait a minute before you go off and blow half of Sega Clan to the nine hells. Just let me think a minute."

Micha stopped and turned back. "Make it good."

Lortax turned to the king. "You have proof there was a plot against Micha."

"Yes, a plot by Sega to kill Micha and me as well. They were also behind the uprising in Arcalia. Too many of the ships that pursued me were Sega ships."

"I'll call him out to face the charges. If he refuses I have an excuse to dig him out."

"He'll run," replied Borad.

"Then Micha can have him," replied Lortax. "Don't mistake me here, people, I'll lose no sleep over the death of Kemge. I just don't want the whole sector to implode over it. He came at Micha, that's Clan Council business. He attempted to overthrow you, that's sector business, my business. Tell me you have proof he was behind the uprising."

"I've collected an entire dossier over the past few days," replied Borad. "You'll have full access to it."

"All right, I'll call him out. Micha, he'll run. There's no way he has enough firepower to risk open battle with my fleet. He'll run, but I have no idea where. It'll be up to you to find him."

"Just keep his forces busy until I do," replied Micha. "Make a show, give me time to track him down." Lortax nodded and Micha walked out of the room.

Deann turned to Lortax. "Viceroy, is there any chance Kemge might try to make a run to safety through the Gap?"

"He might risk it if he thought Micha was on his trail. He'll be flying Arcalian ships now, so as long as he can stay ahead he could make it through."

"Oh no, he'll never make it through. He's never heard of Red Nova so he won't be expecting a welcoming committee."

King Borad chuckled at that. "Oh yes, it is a bad day to be Kemge of Sega."

"Oh?"

"Yes, Viceroy," replied the king. "I've seen Red Nova in battle."

"I've seen them in battle on the ground," said Hawk. "Deann, could you use a decent gunner on your crew?"

"I'd love to have you, Hawk, but Michella will shoot me if I steal any more of her crew. Speaking of Chella, I'd like to catch her before she lifts off." Borad gave her the nod and she left the room.

Deann found Michella supervising the loading of her ship. "You're heading out, too?"

"Yeah. We're all going. This is all crazy, but it is what it is."

"Micha didn't send you home to guard the Gap?"

"You mean to keep me safe. He tried."

"Chella, be careful. Come back to me."

Michella suddenly gave Deann her full attention. "That's a strange thing to hear, especially from you, Dee. What's going on?"

"Get it through your head, pretty woman. I love you, always have, always will. I want you to be safe. Chella, I need for you to be safe."

"Dee, what's going on? What's really going through that head of yours? First you break our bond, bond with another, and now profess undying love for me. I'm confused and hurt here. I understand why you did what you did. I'm trying to get past everything, but I can't, won't be able to if you keep doing this."

Others were looking at them now and Deann was red-faced. Suddenly she stepped into Michella's arms and hugged her tightly. "By all the gods I've missed you, Chella." Suddenly she whispered in Michella's ear then stepped back. "Just come back in one piece, please."

Michella's face wore a look of shock. Her mouth worked but no words came out. Deann kissed her cheek then turned and walked away. "Good hunting," she called, as she headed for the Raptor.

Michella turned and found Alore standing beside her. "What did she say, Chella?"

"Nothing important," sighed Michella, as she shook off the shock.

"Skeeter. I saw her whisper something to you and now you're completely out of focus. What did she say?"

"She said she wants me to come back in one piece."

"I heard that part. What else?"

"She said that, according to the Red Nova histories, the Matriarch had two bonded companions."

"A three way bond? Chella?"

"Happens all the time, 'Lore."

"Well, I know that," she replied tartly. "But you and Dee and ..."

"Yeah, I think that's what I just heard."

"And she told you this just before we launch for a mission that could take months or more."

"Yup."

"That's just Dee all over. She's giving you time to consider it before you shoot her."

"I should shoot her."

"Yes, you should."

"I mean, she came back seven years older, seven times more savage, and seven times ..."

"More desirable?"

"Saw through me, huh? So when did you get so grown up?"

"Last week in the Gap," replied Alore. "Yep, Dee is a force of nature all right."

"Yes, she's that and more. How did that happen? Where is the sweet little girl I brought off Nova Prime?"

"Gone, and it's all your fault."

"My fault? How did it get to be my fault?" asked Michella.

"You got yourself captured. The instant Dee heard you'd been taken off world she took command and went after you. Chella, at no time did anyone on the crew think to argue with or disobey her. They took you and that released the beast. That woman we know now is the result of that. Dee was born to command, to rule. You know it, too."

"Yeah, there's no doubt about that. 'Lore, what should I do? I'm lost here."

"Go sit in the captain's chair and take command of your ship, lead your crew, help Pappa run down and destroy the enemy of Nova."

"And then?"

"Then, and only then, consider what she said."

"Consider what she said? Share her in a three way?"

"Well, you'd have to show old what's his name who's boss lady, but you know, might be fun."

"Alore? Oh my oath, does Mamma know you talk like that? Does she even know you think like that?"

Alore had a twinkle in her eye. "Hormones, Chella. I can't control it at all."

"Well you'd better learn. You're only fifteen, for pity sake."

"I'll be sixteen next month, besides. You can't shoot me for thinking."

"Don't be so sure, missy. Get your buttocks back in that sick bay. And don't think for a moment that I don't know what you just did."

"Did? I didn't do anything." Alore laughed as she danced away from her sister and climbed onto the ship.

"The hell you didn't," grumbled Michella. "You just did a Deann on me." She entered the ship and closed the hatch. "Bridge, get this ship in the air."

"Aye, Captain," came Bim's voice. "Bird rising."

Back on the ground Deann stood watching as the Warbird disappeared into the afternoon sky. Dornal approached and put his arm around her shoulders. "Did you speak to her?"

"I told her."

"What did she say? No, don't tell me, you ran away before she could say anything."

"Dor, if you ever breathe a word about how big a chicken I am, I'll pull out every chest hair you've got, one at a time."

"Not a word," he grinned.

Back to the Gap

Micha had been gone a week before Deann, her ships fully topped up and fully loaded with supplies, headed back towards the Gap. The king had promised the new ships within the year, and she was well pleased. They'd saved the king, thwarted Sega Clan, and Micha was on the hunt for Kemge. Deann felt she had accomplished her goal. Arcalia had not fallen. Nova would retain her supplies and a strong ally. Nine days of uneventful travel later ...

"What's bugging you now?" asked Nellie.

Deann had sat in the captain's chair for hours, brooding over something. "Huh? What?"

"Comms to Captain."

"Sorry, Nellie. My thoughts were elsewhere."

"Out there chasing Kemge with Micha's crew?" asked Dor.

"No, not really. No, I'm trying to get my head around the rest of it. Kemge will come to us if he survives long enough."

"Come to us?" exclaimed Barah as he relinquished pilot to Tanie. "What in the nine hells makes you think he'll come to us?"

"Kemge's no fool," replied Deann. "He was there when the Gap was created. He knows there's no fleet large enough to stop Micha when he has Lady Arlessa and Lady Norlene with him. Kemge saw the destruction of the Imperial forces. No, he'll run. He'll be flying Arcalian ships so he can match Micha's speed, he just has to get out in front of him."

"So?" asked Dor.

"So, he knows no one in Sector Nine will help him against Micha. The only hope he has is in reaching Imperial space."

Barah grinned. "The only way to reach Imperial space is through the Gap. You're right, Dee. So how do we catch him? There're three paths through the Gap. We can't cover them all unless we want to face him with a single ship."

"No, I want the Red Fleet together when we face him. We need an early warning system."

"An early warning system?" said Nellie.

"Yes, Nellie, an early warning system."

"Dee, you're looking at me like that again," said Nellie as she held up a hand defensively. "What are you asking me to do?"

"Nellie, can you do what Ena does?"

"Ena? You mean detect truth or lies? Yes, to a degree. Why?"

"Start practicing. You'll need to be sharp when we reach the Gap."

"All right, you, what are you planning?" asked Nellie.

"The Matriarch began Red Nova within the Pirates. That's where we'll get our early warning system. We need allies with eyes and there's no one else we can turn to."

"Deann, they'll have you over a barrel if you do this. We'll be working for Zemma for the rest of our lives."

"Not if I get this right."

"Dee, what are you planning to do?"

"Adopt Zemma into the clan."

"Have you gone completely crazy?" asked Barah.

"I'm wide open to alternatives. If you've got a better idea, let's hear it."

"Well, why not just spread out warning beacons?"

"Okay, how many do you estimate it will take to give us adequate warning of their approach and their course of travel?"

Barah's shoulders slumped. "About ten ship loads, give or take."

"Ah-huh."

"There has to be another way." Barah started to pace about the bridge. "Dee, put that magic thinking cap on and find a better way. If you bring Zemma before the Clan I'll object. I will."

The bridge was silent. They had never heard anyone speak to Deann that way. No one ever defied her. Her eyes were hard as she rose from the captain's chair to go nose to nose with him. Barah didn't back down. "Come on, Dee. You know you can't trust her. Micha doesn't trust her, Lady Arlessa doesn't trust her, and Ena doesn't trust her."

"Dee, I'd attack the gates of the eighth hell with Red Nova at my back, any one of them. Why? Because I know them, all of them, and I trust them. Any one of them would give his life to protect my back and they know I'd do the same for them. Frankly, I wouldn't eat breakfast with Zemma at my back.

"Look, we're not in a fight or an emergency here. We're cruising through empty space. It's boring. You don't do your best work when there's no action. Put that thinking cap back on and think of something better."

In spite of herself, Deann grinned. "Why don't you go start a fight somewhere so I can think straight?"

"Now you're talking." Barah sighed with relief and the whole bridge crew relaxed. "Dee, I'm sorry, but ..."

"No, Barah, you were right to speak. If you can't accept that idea then I'll put it aside. The trust of the clan is more important. I was just working off Eddan's histories. According to that it was Zemma's crew we melded with to create Red Nova. All right, we'll go at this a different way. If we're destined to blend with Zemma's crew then they'll have to earn our trust. Deal?"

"Deal."

Now it was Deann's turn to pace around the bridge. "All right, here's what I had in mind to start with. Maybe we can still make some of it work. What I wanted to do was enlist Zemma's help to set up a network of ships strung out along the edge of the Gap. I wanted them out into Arcalian space far enough to spot Kemge on sensors and give us enough warning to block him.

"We'd be orbiting the hunting lodge as it's near the center of access points to the Gap crossings. From there we could reach and block whichever entrance he makes for, if we have enough warning. The idea was to make Zemma earn her way into the clan by helping us with this. It could still work, but I'll need to figure out another way to bring her on side."

"I think I might have an idea that would work," said Nellie.

"Talk to me, girl."

"We could offer her a ship, Dee. We'll be getting new ones, better ones that Gold Nova has now."

"And Micha still has two shiny new ships stashed away for emergency use. Nellie, you're a genius. Those ships are witch locked. Can you unlock one?"

"Sure."

"Why not find out what she really wants first?" asked Dor.

"What do you mean?" asked Deann.

"Well, before you give away the farm, why not see what she really wants first?"

Deann smiled ruefully and squeezed his arm. "It's a good thing one of us can think straight when we're bored. You're right, Dor. First thing we need to do is find Zemma and talk her into it without selling ourselves into slavery to the pirates. Sensors."

"Sensors here, Chieftain."

Deann grinned at the older fellow at the sensor station. "Is there anybody out there I can start a fight with to clear my head?"

"Sorry, Chieftain. Nothing there but empty space and more empty space."

"Damn. Dor, take the chair. I'm going down to the exercise area and burn off a bit of steam. Anybody want to work out with me?" There were no takers.

Eight days later, they reached the Gap and found Zemma in a pitched battle. Deann raced to the bridge at the call of Battle Stations. She hopped into the chair. "Report."

"Sixteen ships engaged in heavy fighting. We've been recognized and are being hailed." replied Tanie.

"On screen."

A harried looking Zemma faced the camera. "Deann of Red Nova, I'd like to call in that favor now."

"Move your ships in behind the Red Fleet. Attention all ships, stand down or be destroyed."

"Who the hells do you think you are to be flinging orders," came a voice.

"This is Deann of Red Nova aboard the Raptor. You have ten seconds to stand down or make peace with your maker. This is Nova territory, and I will enforce Novan rule. Stand down."

Eight of the ten ships began to power down their weapons, but two turned and fired on the Raptor. Deann's ship easily twisted out of the way of the incoming missiles and returned fire. Both ships exploded. "Anybody else?" Deann asked over the ship-to-ship comms. All ships were powered down.

"All right. Zemma."

"Zemma here."

"Power down your weapons now. Let me deal with this."

"Understood. Powering down weapons."

"Sensors?"

"All ships are powered down, Chieftain."

"Good. Now, who speaks for the eight ships facing me?"

"This is Argin, aboard the Laris. Listen, Novan, that woman is the worst blood thirsty pirate in the entire galaxy. We were ordered by the agents of the king to clear out this area of space from pirates."

"That's odd, Argin," said Deann. "I just left Arcalia Prime and King Borad said nothing about this to me. I'm sure if he wanted this area cleaned up he'd have asked me to do it. I'm a personal friend, after all."

"Lies, child, all lies. Borad is dead. Goro is king now and he ..."

"Forgive me," replied Deann, still smiling, "but I managed to prevent the death of His Majesty King Borad. He's returned to Arcalia Prime and Goro the Usurper has fled for his life. Now, as I said before, this is Nova Clan territory, and I will enforce Nova rule. Tell me clearly now, who's man are you, Borad's or Goro's?"

"Child, I don't believe a word you say."

Quint's face appeared in the screen. "Deann of Red Nova is our Chieftain and matriarch. Put some respect in your voice if you want to survive. Call her child again and I'll blow your buttocks halfway through the Gap. Please continue, Chieftain."

"Thank you, Captain Quint. All right, Argin. Believe this. If any of you even flinch I'll blow the lot of you to the nine hells. I'm tired of your stupidity. I'll confer with Zemma now. You might spend some time searching for news vids from the past two weeks.

"Zemma."

"Here."

"Permission to come aboard your ship?"

"Of course, Deann. I'll get the lads to tidy her up a bit. Come on over."

"Nice try. Power down now and we'll lock up. Deann out." She signaled for the comms to be cut then headed for the door. "Nellie, you're with me. Dor ..."

"I've got this, Chieftain. Remember, be diplomatic."

"Right, diplomatic. I can do it. Come on, Nellie."

The ships locked up and Deann was waiting for the soft hiss of the air locks. As the doors began to open Nellie shifted into flaming black robes and stepped in front of Deann. Three strides carried her through and into the wall of armed pirates. Nellie thrust out her hand and the men were thrown back against the bulkhead and pinned there. "Drop all weapons," demanded a terrible voice as she increased the pressure. Weapons fell from nerveless fingers, then Nellie lowered her hand and the men fell to the floor.

"Weapons, Zemma?" asked Deann, as she spotted Zemma standing back, a blaster in each hand. One blaster was aimed at Deann and one at her own head.

"I won't wear the slave collar again," she replied, her voice devoid of emotion. "I'll die first. You can have the damned ship."

"Nellie." Nellie's hand shot out and Zemma froze. She was lifted up and floated to Deann who gently relieved her of the blasters. At Deann's nod Nellie released her. "I don't want your ship, woman, and Nova doesn't keep slaves. Come on now, let's go somewhere and talk. This was the emperor's ship, there must be a meeting room somewhere."

Zemma swallowed hard. Her badly scarred face showing confusion and mistrust, her eyes wary. "What do you want?"

"I want your help. So, do you want to talk here or is there someplace you'd be more comfortable. Bring the people you trust as well. Everybody might as well hear this first hand."

Suspicious and fearful, Zemma led the way, signaling for others to join them. Four others fell in behind them, three men and a woman. All were extremely respectful, Nellie had made her point.

The ship was surprisingly clean and tidy. The crew appeared to be well disciplined as well, and there were a lot of them. Deann approved.

They entered the mess hall and Deann grinned. "Hey, your meeting room looks just like ours."

Zemma smiled in spite of herself. "Have a seat, tell me what's on your mind."

"Your ship looks to be in good shape. Crew looks good, too."

"Thanks."

"Zemma, why do you do it?"

"Do it? Do what?"

"What you do. I know you were a slave who broke free, probably killed the master in the process."

"Cut his evil throat from ear to ear," replied Zemma.

"Proper thing," agreed Deann. "So you joined the pirates, worked your way up to Captain, went independent and prospered. Why keep going?"

"Why? Because I have a crew to feed, that's why. This is a great ship and I owe Micha for her to be sure, but she needs fuel, repairs, and the crew needs to eat, clothes and such. We need munitions for the guns and every damn bit of it costs. We can't get honest work, they'd hang us in a heartbeat if they got their hands on us. That's why we do what we do. We steal a cargo and lose half that or more to the fence when we sell it and the rest goes to keep us in the air."

"So that's what it's all about? Staying in the air?"

"Girl, every living soul on this ship is a former slave. We stay in the air, we stay free. We have a good and comfortable life on this ship. All we ask is to keep her in the air, to stay free."

"I get that," sighed Deann. "That's pretty much what we're all about as well. You ever wish you could settle down someplace?"

"No. Where could we go? We all have slave brands and worse. As soon as those were spotted we'd be right back where we started, in chains. No, girl, we'll keep flying, stay free as long as we can.

"Now, are you planning to tell me what's going on or do you want the rest of my sad life story?'

Deann just chuckled, taking no offense. "I don't need your life's story, Zemma. I just needed enough to know if I could trust you."

"You can't. Ask anybody you want, they'll tell you. Zemma's a cold-blooded killer and you can't turn your back on her. Even Micha will tell you that."

"So, you're saying I should just kill you now and have done with it."

"That's the safest way."

Nellie laughed at that. "Zemma, one thing you'll learn is Deann rarely takes the safest route. Dee, What I said before about your plan, forget I spoke." Deann nodded and smiled.

"You know," said Deann, "I noticed a lot of folks on this ship. A bit crowded are you?"

"We're cozy. Not a problem."

"Zemma, you've got children and young mothers on board. Ever thought of finding a little out of the way planet for them?"

"And see the slave raiders get them? Not a chance, girl."

"Is there that much slave raiding this close to the Gap? I thought the king had put a stop to all that."

"It's one thing to pass a law and another to enforce it. Arcalia was spread too thin and so is Nova. Can't be everywhere at once."

"That's the hard truth of it," said Deann. "Okay, I guess it's about time I got to the point of this visit."

"And I thought you just wanted to stop by for dinner."

"I will, Zemma. One day I'll do just that. Right now I have a big problem and I need your help to solve it."

"Oh?"

"Listen, I do understand how hard it is to keep a warship supplied. So, here's what I want you to do and why. I'll pay you with a full load of food, supplies, and munitions. I'll even give you half up front. Do me right here and maybe I can even see you to another ship, something like what Micha's flying."

She had Zemma's attention then. "An Arcalian war ship? Why would you?"

"Because I need you, and as a sign of good faith. I need your trust and I need to be able to trust you. Zemma, I don't want you to go to war for me, I have Red Nova to do that. What I need is this. Right now Micha has gone after Kemge of Sega Clan. Kemge knows he's coming and he'll run. If Micha catches up with him first, then all is well and good. However, I expect that snake to slip by Micha and make a run for Imperial space."

Zemma nodded. "With Micha on his trail that would be his best bet. So the question is, where will he come? Which path through will he make for?"

"Exactly. I can't be everywhere at once."

"So you want me to block up this pathway?"

"No, Kemge will most likely be flying Arcalian warships. You'd be no match for him. No, what I need from you is a network of pi ... people watching for him. They'll have to be out into Arcalian space a bit so they can warn me in time for me to head him off. I'll hang out about midway and wait for the signal."

"Dear gods, woman, to watch the whole Gap will take dozens of ships spread out all along." Zemma stopped and sighed. "You knew that already." Deann nodded. "That'll cost me every favor I'm owed and a bunch more I'll have to come good for."

"I know."

"But you don't care."

"Why should I? What am I, your sister? Truth now. Can you do this?"

"Possibly. Look, if I do this and you ..."

"I swear you'll get your ship."

"Why bother with any of it, girl. Let him go through. Micha will hunt him down in time and no harm done. Keep your ship." Zemma shivered as Deann's eyes hardened.

"Because I want Kemge dead." Deann relaxed and shook off the mood.

"There's more to it than that," said Zemma.

"Yes there is, but the rest can wait. Will you do it?"

"Zemma, a ship like that could make the difference for us," said one of her men.

"I believe her, Zemma," said another. "Nova Clan has always stuck to their word. Who cares why she wants this done? We get a ship like that, and we take no risks. So what if we owe a few favors."

"I hate owing favors. So, you all want to do this?"

"Yes," replied her advisers.

"All right, Deann of Red Nova, we'll take the job. You did say you'd see us to a few supplies first."

Deann grinned and reached for her comms. "Raptor, this is Deann."

"Here, Chieftain."

"Bring half our food supplies and half our munitions to the air lock then stuff them through."

"Chieftain?"

"Do it, Dor."

"Aye, Chieftain. Stuffing supplies through the airlock."

"How's your fuel, Zemma?"

"We're near full up," said the other woman.

"Okay, so you're good for now. Zemma, when this is done right I'll know I can trust you to finish the job you take on. When I deliver that ship you'll know you can trust me to keep my word on payment. We'll build on that when the time comes." She offered her hand to seal the bargain and, reluctantly, Zemma took it.

"All right then, Nellie and I will leave you to it. Once you have the supplies we'll unlock. Now I'll go back and convince those folk who were shooting at you to help you set up the spy network."

"Them? You think you can convince them to help?"

"Sure," grinned Deann. "No problem at all."

"You're crazier than I am, Deann the Giant Killer. Yes, I know who you are. So what's the story on this Red Nova thing?"

"Story for another time, Zemma," said Deann. "I'll tell you over dinner on that new ship when I deliver it."

Deann returned to her own bridge. She waited quietly until the two ships separated then she asked for ship-to-ship comms. "Raptor to Laris."

"Argin here."

"Tell me, Argin, did you get any news while I was away?"

"I did. I owe you an apology. Borad is indeed still king. We will withdraw."

"The hell you will. You even breathe loud and I'll open fire. We're not done here yet."

The man visibly swallowed hard. "What do you want?"

"I want you to pay close attention. Right now I'd be happy to just shoot you, but Zemma has a task for you. Mind your manners, stay respectful, and you'll all live to see another day. Mess with me on this and I'll hunt you down. Are we clear here?"

"Very clear. However, I should point out that Zemma is a cold-blooded killer."

"Yes she is, and I'm twice as bad, so bear that in mind. We're setting up a listening net across the Gap. You will be part of that net. Zemma will give you directions and you won't argue, you'll obey. Clear?"

"Understood, Red Nova. Laris awaiting orders."

"Zemma."

"Here, Deann."

"Happy?"

"Good as I ever get."

"Elgin is the captain of the Laris. Put him and his ships to work then get busy. I'll go see if I can scrounge up a spare ship.

It took two weeks to reach the place where Micha hid the ships. Deann and her captains plus other advisers met on the Raptor each day for a planning session. There was another reason Deann wanted that extra ship. She hoped they would have the time.

The Dragon and the Comet stood guard outside the anomaly while the Raptor slipped inside.

"Man, that freaks me every time," said Barah.

"Yeah, gave me the dizzies too," agreed Tanie.

"All right, we're here," said Deann. "I still see two ships. Nellie, you ready?"

"Ready, Dee. Can I have my favorite pilot?" Deann smiled. "Barah, you're with Nellie. Tanie, on pilot. Nellie, take a few more with you for crew."

"Understood."

A few moments later a small fighter ship launched and approached the two silent ships. Deann watched and nervously waited. "It's taking too long," she muttered. Finally the hatch opened and the fighter slipped inside the silent ship. Shortly the engines came to life and the interior lights could be seen.

Nellie's sexy purr sounded over the comms. "Raptor, this is the Spellbinder, Nellie of Red Nova commanding. Awaiting orders, Chieftain."

"Nellie, you're the best. Okay, bring her out and we'll head back towards the king's hunting lodge."

"Understood." The ship rose gracefully and followed the Raptor back out of the anomaly.

Once outside they headed for open space, moving in the general direction of the hunting lodge. Suddenly the man on comms turned to Deann. "Chieftain, I'm getting strange messages directed to the Raptor from unknown ships."

"Messages? What do they say?"

"Just three words. No sightings yet."

Deann grinned her delight. "That means Zemma's getting her network in place. Keep monitoring that and let me know the instant they have a sighting."

"Understood." He turned back to the station panel.

Blocking the Path

O nce they were well away from the anomaly they stopped and spread out. Barah made several attack runs at each of the superior ships and each time they easily slipped in behind him. Finally Deann was satisfied and the ships came back together.

"You've all got the idea now," said Deann as she met with her captains. "You know where to hit them to cripple them without killing them."

"The thing I still don't understand," said Quint, "is why we don't just blow them to the nine hells?"

"I think I've got that one figured out," said Girta, a smile playing at her lips. "The chieftain wants their ships."

"Deann laughed with delight. "Keep going, Girta."

"You want the ships for Zemma. She was flying old battered ships beside one good one. She's probably got over a hundred people on those old rust buckets."

"But why?" asked Quint.

"They're the ancestors, Quint," replied Girta. "Right, Eddan?"

"Yes. Deann of Nova and the four were the true warriors, but they blended with the pirates, and we're the results. Yes, they're the ancestors. Is that why you're trying to help them, Matriarch?"

"That would be it," sighed Deann.

"Well, skeet, sorry I messed with you on that one, Dee," said Barah.

"No, your objection was valid. I was probably getting in a hurry. They do need to earn their place with us. We can make it a bit easier by providing them with opportunities, but they do need to work for it. A loose alliance with Zemma is the best for now. I want to keep an eye out for them, but they need to be strong in their own right if they're to be the ancestors of Red Nova." The others nodded their agreement.

"Okay, once we have them dead in space what happens?"

"They'll launch small fighters, those we can blow out of the sky," replied Deann. "I want Kemge to be here to face Micha himself so we knock down their engines because we don't know which ship will be his."

"But he's a coward," grinned Pally, "so he won't be in one of the fighters."

"Now we just have to wait and hope he shows up," said Eddan. "Matriarch, I do believe there's something else going on here. Wait, the usurper, the king said he'd flee to his friend, Kemge. You're hoping to capture him as well."

Deann was grinning her delight. "Yes, indeed I am. The king already owes us, and he will deliver, but if we can send him the usurper as an extra gift ..."

"It'll increase the bond between Arcalia and Red Nova," said Alise. "Captain Deann, I like the way your mind works. Always you strive to make the clan stronger, to protect the people."

They were interrupted then. "Bridge to Chieftain."

"Go ahead."

"Message received from Zemma. All is in place. Nothing yet."

"Acknowledged."

"So now we wait," said Dor.

"And now we wait." said Deann.

They waited, plotted, planned, and trained. Deann realized Barah had been right, without action to occupy her she got lost. She couldn't afford to do that now. Daily she played with the children, trained her body, her troops, and her ships. After about three weeks a convoy of ships appeared out of the Gap. She went after them.

"Convoy, this is Deann of Red Nova, power down your ships and weapons. You're in Nova territory. Identify."

"Deann, is that you? It's Kella. Where's Micha? What's happened? Who or what is Red Nova?"

"Whoa, easy, woman. Yes, this is Deann. Come aboard and I'll bring you up to speed. Hold your convoy steady until we've talked."

"Deann, tell me you're not going to rob my convoy."

"Trust me," grinned Deann. "Come on over."

Kella's speeder was soon aboard, and she was escorted to the kitchens where Deann was waiting. "Deann, what's happened to you?" asked Kella. "You look older, and a lot scarier."

"I am older and scarier, Kella. Sit and I'll tell you a story." Deann told her of the time ship and finding Red Nova. She told of her years there, their escape, saving the king and all that happened since.

"Wow, I'm gone for a few months and everything changes completely. So, you're in charge of the Gap now?"

"Temporarily until Micha gets back."

"And you're hoping to catch Kemge for him?"

"That I am. You can tell your convoy to go ahead, but be on the watch for Kemge. I want to know the minute they sight him if they do. The pirate network is too spread out to give you any trouble."

"Thanks for that," said Kella. "So, what's the plan for after Micha returns?"

"After that I try to fit my clan into the Novan people, but on my own terms. If I can't, I'll be looking for a home for them."

"Have you given any thought to mercenary work? My convoys could always use more protection."

Deann laughed. "I'll think about it. Basically, I told you what I did so you could keep your folks out of the line of fire. Also, the Guild will all need to know to avoid trouble with Red Nova. If they ever encounter one of our ships they need to mind their manners."

"Duly noted. Thanks Deann."

"Welcome. Now I'm going to do you another favor."

"Oh?"

I know you're aware of who Zemma is."

"Oh yeah. The thoughts of her give me the creeps. She's a cold-blooded killer and an efficient pirate. If you could take her out of the action I could do business is a number of planets I have trouble reaching now. I haven't even tried since Michella backed her up last year."

"Go back into the area, but send out messages to her first. Offer her food, fuel, and munitions for two ships in exchange for her leaving Guild ships off her hit list."

"Now there's a nice dream."

"Tell her I sent you and that I said she should take the deal. She'll listen."

"Are you sure?"

"Dead sure. She'll listen or I'll make her listen."

"All right, what's this going to cost me?"

"Saw through me, huh?"

"Oh yeah. Talk to me, Deann of Red Nova."

"Kella, you have a network of people all through Sector Nine. If anyone even breathes like they're going to have a go at Arcalia or Nova, I want to know the minute they think it."

"You want access to my spy network," said Kella. "Fair enough. Is that all?"

"That's all for me. Take your convoy through, but keep an eye out for Kemge. Let me know if you see him."

"Count on it. Deann, It's good to be on friendly terms again. You know I had nothing to do with what happened to Michella."

"I know, Kella. That was Ayra's doing, and it was personal. I'd have handled it differently."

"Oh, what would you have done?"

"I'd have killed her the minute she got in my face."

Kella shivered at the hard look in Deann's eye. "I believe you."

Kella went on her way but a few hours later a message was relayed to the Raptor. One of the pirates had spotted the quarry and relayed the message through Kella's convoy. Kemge was two weeks out and headed right to the first entry point to the Gap. Deann recalled her crew from the Spellbinder and set out to head him off. The Spellbinder was left orbiting around the hunting lodge planet. Deann sent a coded message to Zemma. "Job well done. Your payment is where I was hiding." Zemma would understand.

Red Nova headed out at full burn; there was no time to lose. The next day they got an update. Twenty Arcalian warships were inbound at full burn, pursued by three more. Red Nova arrived at the entry point first and set up a blockade. There was no way around them. Another report reached them. The twenty ships would arrive in eighteen hours, the trailing three in two days. Deann ordered all ships shut down to minimum so everybody could get a full rest period before the excitement started.

Deann was awake early as usual. A quick workout, then a stop to play with the kids for a while and then to the mess hall for a meal. Many of the crew were there and there was a lot of excitement and speculation. Deann was smiling as she listened to them. They were well trained and ready for anything.

She finished her meal then headed for the bridge. "Sensors," she said, as she took her place in the captain's chair.

"We have the twenty ships on sensors now, Captain. There are three blips way back but keeping pace with the twenty."

"That'll be Gold Nova. All right, people, get ready. Comms, sound battle stations." The klaxon sounded, but there was no need, all hands were already at their stations.

"They're coming in hard, Chieftain. We're sitting still."

"I know, Dor. Patience now." Deann waited a few minutes longer, then gave the order to move. "Fleet, ahead one half speed."

"Ahead one half, aye," replied Barah. He was at his favorite station, pilot.

"Comms, hail the oncoming ships."

"Hailing ships, aye. No response, Chieftain."

"Give me ship-to-ship."

"Ship-to-ship, aye."

"Attention, oncoming ships, you are entering Nova Clan space. Power down your ships and identify." No response. "Identify or be destroyed."

"Get out of the way you moronic cow or you'll be the one getting destroyed. I don't know who you are, nor do I care. That's Nova Clan behind me, so you're no more than an irritant."

"That's better." Deann was grinning and Dor shivered to see the look in her eye. "Now, Kemge of Sega, I'm Deann of Red Nova, and if you think those people on your trail are dangerous, let me enlighten you. They're nothing compared to Red Nova. Power down or pay the price."

There was no response from the ships, but the woman on sensors spoke. "Chieftain, one of the ships has dropped back behind the others."

"That'll be Kemge's ship. Fleet, attack speed."

Kemge's ship dropped back behind his guards, and he gave the order to fire. It was too late; the Red fleet was already at attack speed. The warriors on Kemge's ships were horrified at the speed of the Novan ships. They fired a full barrage but scored not one single hit. Red Nova managed to disable several ships as they wove their way through the small fleet. They turned back and came in again so quickly the remaining ships barely had time to turn to face them.

It didn't help, several more ships suffered damage to their engines. In desperation the ships spilled out their small fighter ships. Red Nova followed suit. There were several dozen small fighters against the fourteen Nova could field, but the results were the same. As soon as the battle was joined it was clear the Sega fighters were no match for the faster and more agile fighters of the Novans. As their numbers were dramatically cut, the Sega fighters struggled to return to the bigger ships.

Red Nova collected her fighter ships then turned and retreated to the mouth of the Gap. "Comms, ship-to-ship," said Deann.

"Ship-to-ship, aye. Go ahead, Chieftain."

"Kemge of Sega, are we having fun yet? What have you got left, six functional ships? No? Not even that many? You should have listened to me." She turned to Dor. "Attack plan B."

"Plan B, aye," he replied, grinning. He reached for the comms on his shoulder and she returned to the ship-to-ship screen.

"Kemge of Sega, talk to me now. Don't make me do this the hard way. Nova Crew is inbound about fourteen hours out."

"What do you want?"

"Now we're getting somewhere. What I want to start with, is for your ships to power down the weapons before I lose my temper."

A moment later sensors spoke again. "They're powering down, Captain. All but one."

"Does that one still have engines?"

"I believe so, Chieftain. They're turning on thrusters only, but they're angling for open space." Deann nodded.

"Kemge, power down. Now. Don't even think about making a run for it. I'll just chase you down, destroy your engines, then leave you there for Nova Crew. Power down." She looked to sensors then nodded. "Good boy."

"What do you want?"

"Goro the Usurper. I believe you have him on your ship, do you not?"

"I have no idea what you're babbling about."

"No? Well then, we'll just wait for Micha to get here then he can help me search your ships. Won't that be fun?" At that the remaining functional five Sega ships scattered, each going in a different direction.

"Run them down," shouted Deann. "Run them down. Disable them."

The three Nova ships gave chase, ignoring the two which had turned in the general direction Micha was coming from. Of the remaining three, one headed away from the opening to the Gap. The Dragon went after it. The Comet went after another, and the Raptor went after the last. It took them a while, but they managed to run them down and disable them.

The Raptor turned to face her victim. "Deann of Red Nova to facing ship. Talk to me or I'll blow you to hell and back."

"This is Captain Sagan. We surrender. Do not fire, we surrender."

"Show me Kemge of Sega Clan and the Usurper, Goro."

"They're not on this ship."

"Fire."

"Wait, wait, they're not on this ship. Board us, search all you want. They're not on this ship." Deann gave a jerk of her head and the Raptor turned away and headed back.

"Comet to Raptor."

"Go ahead, Quint."

"There's a man here who wants to talk to you, Chieftain. He says he has something you want."

"On my way." Deann was smiling with delight. "Sensors, what about the other two ships?"

"Destroyed, Chieftain. Gold Nova seems to be in a bad mood."

Deann chuckled at that. She had Kemge and the usurper. All was well. Gold Nova was within hailing distance by the time she reached the Comet. "Ravage to Raptor."

"Raptor here. Welcome back, Ravage."

"Report."

"There were a number of ships attempting to rush the Gap, Micha. Some person named Kemge of Sega seemed to be in charge. He's waiting for me beside the Comet right now. Shall I detain him for you?"

"Please do. Ravage out."

The Raptor settled in close to the Comet. "Ship-to-ship."

"Ship-to-ship, aye."

"Kemge, you there?"

"I've got what you want, now let me go."

"Show me." A terrified man was suddenly hauled before the screen. He had been beaten. "Put him in a suit and kick him out the air lock. I'll reel him in."

Kemge disappeared for a moment. The airlock on his ship suddenly opened and a figure reluctantly floated out into space. A fighter from the Raptor launched and pulled him in. "I've done what you ask, now help me. I'll make you richer than you could ever imagine. Take me on board and get me out of here."

"Rich? How are you supposed to make me rich? Your clan and all its wealth is behind you facing an angry viceroy."

"I have friends and connections on the Imperial side. They're planning an attack here. I'll have ten times the power that fool in Arcalia had. Hurry, Micha is almost here."

"All right. Put on a suit and come out, we'll reel you in."

A few moments later a figure pushed off from the damaged ship. The fighter from the Raptor pulled him in then returned to the mother ship. A few minutes more and the comms squawked. "Brig to bridge."

"Bridge here. Are our guests all tucked in?"

"Indeed they are, Chieftain," chuckled the voice. "Two in the brig. We're locked down and clear. Brig out."

"Comms, hail the Ravage."

"Ravage here."

"Micha, I have Kemge and the usurper in my brig. What do you want me to do with the rest of them?"

"Do whatever you want, Deann. I just want Kemge."

"Understood. Raptor to Warbird."

"Bird here. You've been busy, Dee."

"Yep. Chella, I have the usurper in my brig. Do you think King Borad would like to send someone to fetch him?"

"Just so happens I have a direct line to the king. I'll let you know." A few moments later Michella came back on the comms. "The king would be delighted to send a transport for your guest, Dee. Want to lock up or should we meet somewhere?"

"Let's meet at the hunting lodge. I'll deliver my passengers into the hands of Gold Nova as soon as I get there. Right now I want to deal with this mess we have here." The Gold Nova ships turned as one and headed for the hunting lodge. They were desperate for food supplies and that's where they'd find them.

Deann turned back to her comms. "Attention all disabled ships. This is Deann of Red Nova. Have any of you got any fight left in you, or are we finished here?"

Only one voice responded. "We've all surrendered. What are you going to do with us?"

"My first thought is to destroy the lot of you. However, I have business elsewhere. If you can make repairs you are free to go your own way, just leave me two of those ships.

"I expect the Viceroy is looking for you, but that's not my problem. I caution you, however, don't enter the Gap. If I find you in there, there'll be no mercy and no prisoners. In future there will be no mercy, no surrender. If you come at Nova you won't go home. Do you understand?"

"Understood."

"Then I leave you to it." Deann gave the signal to cut the comms. "All right, Barah. Take us to the hunting lodge."

"Aye, Chieftain. New course laid in and transmitted to the fleet."

"Fleet, ahead full."

"Ahead full, aye," said Dor as the ship leaped forward. "Dee, why the rush?"

"I want to catch Micha first, just in case Zemma is still in the area."

"Ah-huh. That the only reason?"

"Shut up, Dor."

"Aye, Matriarch, shutting up now." Deann sighed and rolled her eyes as everybody on the bridge snickered.

The next day they caught up to Gold Nova. They all slowed just enough to let Deann cross to the Ravage in a small fighter. Barah and Nellie were with her. As they landed and descended from their small ship, Rathbone was waiting for them. "They in the kitchen?" asked Deann.

"Where else?" He grinned. "Come on."

Micha and Nova crew were gathered in the kitchen waiting for her. With a grin of pure mischief and a twinkle in her eye, Deann spoke first. "Micha, report." That brought a round of laughter and Micha's was the loudest.

"Aye, Chieftain," he managed as he got his breath back. "We left Arcalia right behind the Viceroy. I expected Kemge to run to his stronghold, but he didn't. While I sat listening to Lortax rattle his saber at Sega Clan, that snake Kemge slipped around me. An old friend of Kella's tipped me off that Kemge had slipped away and I went after him. He had forty ships with him, all Arcalian warships like this one.

"Half of them dropped back to stop me. By the time we fought our way through he had a five day lead on me. We managed to cut that to two days by not stopping to refuel or take on supplies. I hoped to drive him into the Gap where we know the routes better, hoping to get him before he hit Imperial space. It could take years to run him down there. Lucky thing you happened to be in the right place when he arrived.

"Your turn now, report."

Deann grinned her delight. "There was no luck involved. It was hard work and planning. We left Arcalia and returned to the Gap as planned. First I tracked down Zemma and worked out a deal."

"Zemma? What has she got to do with all this?"

"Patience, Chieftain of Gold Nova, I'm getting there." That brought another round of chuckles. "Zemma was key to my plan, and I needed her on side. We worked out a deal. Zemma then organized a network of people she knows, called in favors, offered up a few, made some threats, and the result was a wide loose network of ships just inside Arcalian space watching for Kemge. While we waited we trained and planned. We got the message of twenty ships inbound with three in pursuit headed for number one pathway through the Gap. We hurried on to greet them."

"End result, we have Kemge and Goro in our brig."

Lady Arlessa smiled with admiration. "Deann, that was a masterful plan well executed. I'm impressed."

"I want to know what it's going to cost me," said Micha. He too was grinning.

"Oh, no problem," replied Deann easily. "I've already paid Zemma. She's happy enough."

Micha shook a finger at her. "Deann, what did you give Zemma? Don't give me that wide-eyed little girl look, I'm a grandfather, I can see right through that. Now talk, young woman."

Deann cringed away from him, grinning wickedly. "I gave her one of your spare ships."

"You what? How did you manage to get into ... Nellie."

Nellie was giggling. "Uncle Micha, be careful of your blood pressure. Yes, I opened up the ship for her."

"Dammit, Lessa, I can't leave these kids alone for a minute." He shook his head and grinned. "Talk to me, Dee. Tell me all about it. I know those ships are going to be obsolete soon. It was well done, all of it. Now, tell us what you're holding back about Zemma."

Deann shook her finger at Ena, then sighed. "We need Zemma. The Gap is just too damn big, even for our combined clans, to police. In another time and place, apparently I got sulky and left Nova Clan with a few friends, joined up with Zemma, eventually took over, and Red Nova was the eventual result.

"I've been on Zemma's ship, it's clean and well run, her crew is disciplined, but overcrowded. They're all escaped or rescued slaves. They live as pirates, but everything they steal is sold to make repairs and to buy fuel and supplies. She says, and I believe her, it's all about staying free. Keep flying and you stay free. I needed the help, and she needs the ship.

"I also owe her a few supplies. However, I have Kemge and Goro in my brig and I know that somebody on the imperial side is planning an attack on sector nine."

"Seriously? An attack? Does it never stop?" asked Micha. "Mind if I come over to your ship and see if I can talk Kemge into sharing a little more information?"

"Be my guest."

"Chella, have Hawk get messages to the king and viceroy. We'll update them as soon as we have more information."

"Understood." Michella hadn't spoken, but she'd been watching Deann carefully. Deann had also been stealing glances at her. "I'll return to the Warbird and get that in motion right now. Dee, I want a word in private with that companion of yours."

"Now?" Deann was wide eyed.

"Now. On the Bird."

"Okay," breathed Deann, reaching for her comms. "Deann to Raptor."

"Raptor here."

"Dor, take a fighter and hop over to the Warbird. Chella wants to talk to you."

"Understood Chieftain. I'll pick up a security detail and be on my way. Raptor out."

It was Michella's turn to be wide eyed. "Does he seriously think ...?"

"No, Chella, he's teasing. He's always teasing. The man drives me crazy."

"There was genuine warmth in your voice there, Deann," said Arlessa.

"Yeah, he grows on you," replied Deann. "Dor's a real savage in battle but outside that, he never stops teasing unless he's mad. Don't make him mad, Chella. It's not a pretty sight. Let's go folks. Kemge has a story to tell." She led the way back to her fighter and returned to the Raptor with Micha and most of Nova Crew. Keira and Brenna went with Michella to her ship. As they approached they saw a single fighter leave the Raptor and head towards the Warbird.

Sorting it Out

Deann led the way to the brig. She stepped through the door and instantly was on the receiving end of Kemge's wrath. He'd been taken out of his cell for the interrogation. "You there, slave woman. Get your useless buttocks up to the bridge and bring me that slut of a lying captain. I want ..." He got no further as the security guard felled him with a single blow. Micha was impressed as the young woman security guard was about the same age and size as Alore. Alore couldn't have knocked such a big man down with a single blow like that.

The girl grabbed Kemge by the scruff and hauled him to his knees before Deann. "This woman is the Matriarch. You will speak when she commands it and only when she commands it. When you're required to speak, human, put some respect in your voice, or I will."

As Kemge looked at Deann for the first time and saw the heavily armed, battle scarred, warrior walking towards him he shuddered. "Good job, Linnee," said Deann. "Keep an eye on that other one now. Nova Crew will deal with this one. He's all yours, Micha."

Kemge started to speak, but the girl grabbed his shirt and choked him off with it. "Were you asked to speak? No? Then be silent."

"Thank you, young woman," smiled Arlessa. "I'll take over for you now." She thrust out her hand and Kemge was lifted into the air, gasping for breath. She thrust him hard against the bulkhead and slowly approached, a cold deadly smile playing at her lips. Lessa blew a powder in his face as she released him. He gasped in a deep breath, inhaling the powder as he did. The light of reason left his eyes as he sank to the floor. "He's all yours, Micha."

"Can we record this, Dee?" asked Micha. She nodded at Linnee who grinned and flipped a switch. Micha continued. "Kemge, did you organize the attempt on King Borad's life?"

"Yes."

"Why?"

"Borad's a fool. He has the best ships and the richest resources in the sector, yet he does nothing."

"What should he do?"

"Expand. He should have joined the emperor. I would have and did."

"Yes, you did. Did you send men to kill me?"

"Yes."

"Why?"

"You're too dangerous to keep alive. The Gap needs to be open to all travel."

"Is there a plan from imperial space to invade sector nine?"

"Yes."

"Are you involved with the plan?"

"Yes."

"Why?"

"I'll be governor of Sector Nine. All of it. I can hang that fool Lortax and take full control."

"What is your part in the plan?"

"I have to clear the pathway through the Gap, then when Lortax comes to fight I move my forces in behind him. Finish him. With Lortax dead and his fleet defeated the rest of the clans will fall." Kemge sat drooling as the drug held him in thrall.

"Tell me how you pass messages to those on the other side of the Gap."

"The Trader's Guild carries the messages for me."

"Kella is involved?"

"No. That woman is too stupid to be trusted. She's Lortax's pawn and loyal to him and Nova Clan. No, two of her members were imperial spies for Emperor Loran. When his plot to steal a spawn child failed they were cut off. They came to me looking for work. Spying is what they do."

"So they put you in touch with someone on the other side?"

"Yes, the new CEO of RIM Enterprises."

"RIM still exists?"

"Oh yes," he giggled, and slobbered. "The company never died. It has arisen and taken control of much of its old territory. I'll get Sector Nine once I destroy Arcalia and start the wars again."

"Give me a full list of all the people working with you on this project." He named eleven people including one highly placed Captain in the Viceroy's fleet.

Micha sighed and allowed his shoulders to slump. "Send a copy of that off to the Viceroy and the king. Toss that piece of misery back into a cell. He'll face a trial when we get to the hunting grounds."

"A trial?" asked Deann.

"Trial by combat," growled Micha, as he rose and left the room. Deann nodded to Linnee who grabbed Kemge by the collar and dragged him back into a cell. Deann pointed at Goro, too, and the girl tossed him back into the adjoining cell.

———◆———

ONCE ABOARD THE WARBIRD, Dor made his way to the kitchens with Ellie as guide. His security guard soon disappeared and he was alone with the witch. Dor retrieved a container of water then returned to sit facing her. "The resemblance between you and Priestess Nellie is remarkable, or the resemblance to her the first time I saw her."

"But no longer?"

Dor smiled gently. "She's carried the weight of Red Nova for nearly eight years now," he said. "She's had her trials." A quick grin creased his lips.

"I'll bet she has," replied Ellie, smiling in spite of herself.

"You're not going to turn me into a toad if your captain gets angry are you?"

This time her smile broadened. "I just might, so watch yourself, mister. So, why are you here?"

"I was summoned."

Ellie reached over to grasp his hands and gaze deeply into his eyes. "Just what do you want here, mister Red Nova?"

"First, what will make our matriarch happy. Second what's best for Red Nova. Third what's best for all Novans."

"Good speech, now answer the question."

"I just did, Little Priestess. I just did. Deann spends every moment trying to make things better for the clan. What I can't get through her head is that a healthy, happy, matriarch is best for the clan. She takes nothing for herself."

"Again, good speech. Now answer the question before I turn you into a toad. What do you want for yourself?"

Dor sighed elaborately. "Gods, you're as tough as Priestess Nellie. All right, Little Priestess. For me personally I want a happy Deann. When she's happy my world is bright, my heart sings, and I'm complete. However, that is a rare thing. Too rare."

"So, I ask again, why are you here?"

"I repeat, I was summoned."

"You're up to something, mister. However, I can sense no ill intent in you." She released his hands and sat back.

"I have none, Priestess Ellie. I bring no hurt to your captain, for if I did it would hurt Deann and that I'll never do."

Ellie nodded then stood up. "I believe you, Dornal of Red Nova. Here comes Chella now. Be nice." She turned and walked away.

Dor watched as Michella strode into the room. Her movements were fluid grace and completely confident as she retrieved water then came to sit facing him. "We meet again," he said, as he offered his hand. "I'm Dornal of Red Nova."

"I know who you are," she replied, ignoring his hand. He retrieved it and sat back while she took his measure. "Where's your security guard?"

"Alas, their grandmothers saw us coming and took them captive. I'm alone and at your mercy I fear."

Michella smiled and shook her head. "You brought the kids. Nice touch, but it won't help you with me."

"It wasn't meant to. It was meant to keep the grandmothers from killing me before we had a chance to talk. I warn you, Michella, I'm completely mercenary."

"The hell you are, mister. If you were Ellie would still be here at this table." She sighed and let her shoulders slump. "It's just not fair. I had less than two years with her, and you've had nearly eight."

"I know. She's mourned the loss of you for all eight." Michella looked up at him. "Woman, Dee has never forgotten you, not for a single moment."

"And you're all right with this?"

"I knew from the first it would be this way. I knew she'd never forget you, and I knew it before I bonded with her."

"But you bonded with her anyway."

"Of course I did. The woman is magnificent; do I look like a fool?" She almost laughed at that. "Michella, we had no idea when we'd get out of that ship, or if we ever would. Nor did we know what time period we would be in when we did break free. It wasn't until we were nearly ready to make the break that Dee figured it out, and that broke her heart."

"What do you mean?"

"She knew then she'd come back to your time, older, wiser, and encumbered with a mate, children, and a clan. In her mind she could never return to you, and she knew what that would do to you. Dee will put Red Nova first every time, no matter the cost to herself."

"Yes, she will. She's like my father that way. Being the chieftain is never the easy job if you do it right, so he says, and I believe him." She was quiet for a while, and he didn't disturb her thoughts. Finally she spoke again. "So, in your history, the matriarch had two bonded companions and you think this is the best solution here."

"It is the best solution, Michella, you know that, too. However, I did make that part up."

"Sadly it may just be ... wait, what did you just say? You made it up? You lied to Deann about ..."

"Yep, that I did. She'll shoot me if she ever finds out. My fate is now in your hands, girl."

"Why you misbegotten, miserable son of a ... wait a minute. Oh no you don't, mister. You're not doing that to me."

"What? Doing what? Woman, I didn't ..."

"Oh yes, you bloody well did. Deann does that to me all the time and now Alore has started. I won't put up with it from you too."

"I have no idea at all what you're talking about. I ..."

"The hell you don't. You slipped in a ringer to change my state when you saw me getting depressed and emotional. I know what you did there."

"Damn, you're good." He was grinning at her, and she smiled in spite of herself.

"I really wanted to hate you, you know."

"I know. I didn't want to like you either, but then I saw you and ..."

"Oh shut up, you fool." She was laughing now, and he grinned with delight.

"Dornal, did you really make that up about the two companions?"

"My friends call me Dor. Yes, I did. It's the only solution where Deann gets to be happy and both of us don't die of loneliness or depression. It's not about either of us now, Michella. It's about Deann."

"I know you're right, Dor. Friends call me Chella. However, there is one small problem with all this. Before a priestess will witness a three way bond it has to be a fully loving relationship for all three. I don't know if I can ..."

"Well, you never know until you try it, right? You might like it and ..."

Her mouth had formed a perfect O. She tried to respond but no words came out. And then she saw the grin playing at the corners of his mouth and the merriment in his eyes. "Oh my gods, Dee was right. You're pure evil. I ought to ..." She reached over and slapped his arm hard. That blow would have felled a normal human, but he only burst out laughing.

Michella leaped to her feet and reached for him. Dor tried to cringe away, but she hauled him to his feet and, to his complete surprise, kissed him firmly. Their lips parted slowly then she pushed him away. "Well, at least that finally shut you up, and I didn't drop dead of poison. I guess there's hope."

She placed her hands on his chest and gazed into his eyes. "Stop playing now and be serious. Are you completely committed to this?"

He pulled her close and hugged her gently. Pulling out a chair he seated her facing him again. "I am. You know damn well I am, or I'd never have suggested it in the first place. I had what I wanted, why the hell would I willingly share it unless there was no other way."

"But you don't need another way. You have what you want. Why Dor? I'm serious now, I need to know."

He sat back in his chair and sighed. "I see the pain in your eyes when you look at her, Chella. I see the pain and heartbreak there. I see the same pain in her face when she looks at you. However, she looks at me and I see the love there. She wouldn't be able to fake that with me, it's real. Dee's not complete without you. You're not complete without her, and I'm not complete unless she's happy.

"Now that I've met you, and talked to you, I can see the incredible woman Barah warned me about all those years ago. I see now why Dee can't let you go, and I'm way too selfish to let her go, so there's only really one answer."

"You're a crazy man, you know that?" Chella was smiling at him now and reached for his hand.

"I've heard that before. So, how about it, amazing lady. Help me make the matriarch a happy woman?"

"I've had several months to wrap my head around the idea. The only unknown was us, could we be friends? I think we can, Dor. Oh gods, what if Dee won't ..."

"We'll just have to gang up on her."

Michella smiled. "She'll beat the stuffings out of the both of us, you know that."

"Oh yeah, I know. Chella, we've got some time yet before we reach the hunting lodge. Think about it. If you don't ..."

"Hush now," she replied, placing a finger against his lips. "You're not getting out of it now, mister. After all, it was your idea."

"You're going to use that confession against me, aren't you?"

"Every chance I get, buddy. Every chance I get."

She was smiling now and so was he. "So, we're good here?"

"We are, Dor. We're good. I have no idea at all how this'll all work out, but we're good. Gather up your security team and go home to our girl."

He nodded then hugged her gently again before starting away. "You want to contact her and let her know I survived?"

Michella's delighted laughter followed him out of the mess hall and down the passageway. He reached the infirmary to hear the happy squeals of children and the chatting voices, and he smiled. It was such a wonderful sound. Dor stuck his head through the door and gave the order. "Security detail, mount up, we're going home."

Alise and Leen began to gather the children with Keira and Brenna's help. Ellie pulled Dor aside. "All went well?"

"I believe it did. Barah told the truth when he said she's a magnificent woman. I like her."

"Well done, sir, you survive another day."

Dor gazed into Ellie's eyes for a long moment. "What eats at your soul, Little Priestess?" She didn't reply, just gazed up at him with watery eyes. Dor pulled her into a hug. "Life rarely is what we'd prefer, girl. All we can do is make it work for us as best we can."

Ellie pulled back and gazed up at him again. He took her small shoulders in his hands. "Ellie, I don't know what's eating at you, but one thing I do know for certain. If you don't ask, the answer will always be no." She squeezed his arm tightly then smiled and nodded.

As he ushered his crew back towards the launch bay she turned back to seek out Michella. "Everything okay, Chella?"

Michella was smiling as though the weight of a world had been lifted from her shoulders. "You know, Ellie, I believe it is, or it will be. As crazy as it all sounds, I think his man's mad scheme is going to work. I actually like the guy."

"That's all I need to hear." With that, she left and went to the bridge.

Hawk was on comms and she leaned across his shoulder. In spite of himself he inhaled deeply of her scent. As her cheek touched his he stiffened. He started to turn, but she stopped him. "Hush now, don't say a single word." She whispered in his ear and his eyes went wide. He turned to face her with a look that was a cross between amazement and terror. "Stay right there. I'm going to talk to Noonie now."

"Noonie?" He gasped as he leaped to his feet and tried to follow her.

A barked order stopped him in his tracks. "Get back to your station, Mister. You haven't been relieved." Hawk turned to see Old Rath grinning at him from the Captain's chair and pointing at the comm station. Slowly he returned to the seat at the comm panel.

"I'm dead," he muttered. "I am so dead."

"Oh stop whining," grinned Rath, "you'll go out happy." There was a round of chuckles at that. Hawk just groaned and sank deeper into his chair.

DEANN SAT IN THE KITCHEN, aka mess hall, sipping on some tea and lost in thought. Eddan came in, picked up tea for himself then joined her. "Chieftain," he said, as he raised his mug of tea to his lips.

"Eddan." They sat in companionable silence for a time. Each lost in their own thoughts. It was Deann who finally spoke. "Eddan, I'm curious. Why did you not ever mention that the matriarch had two bonded companions?"

"Two companions? I don't recall anything in the histories about two companions. What made you think you, I mean the historical you, had two bonded companions?"

"Dor said he remembered it from the histories. He was so sure that ... Oh, that man. Excuse me, Eddan. I have a man to shoot." She rose and strode purposefully from the room.

Eddan took another sip of his tea. "Two companions? I wonder whatever made Dor think she had two companions?"

Dor was in the captain's cabin, reading, when she found him. One look at the fire in her eyes and he knew something was up. "Dor, give me one good reason not to shoot you."

For an answer he stood, pulled her close then kissed her. It was gentle and loving at first, but he soon began to put some passion into it. With a soft moan Deann responded in kind. Within moments they were tearing at each others clothes.

Their passion spent, they lay entwined on the bed, her head resting on his chest, listening to his heart beat. He smiled and kissed the top of her head. "So, was that a good enough reason not to shoot me?"

"Barely." She sighed then poked him in the ribs. "You lied to me, Dor. You tricked me into suggesting to Chella that I was supposed to have two bonded companions. I don't like being lied to, and now I'm feeling ashamed and embarrassed. What if she finds out? How can I ever look her in the eye again?"

"She knows."

Deann rose up on one elbow to look him in the eye. "She knows? How could she know?"

"I told her. She said you'd shoot me."

"She's not wrong. Dor, why would you do this? Why would you suggest I take a second companion? Please talk to me. Tell me the truth. Why did you do this?"

He kissed her forehead then sighed as he gazed into her eyes. "Because you were so damned unhappy, Dee, and because, in spite of that, I couldn't bear the thought of being without you. And then there's Michella. She's completely tormented too. I like her, you love her, and you love me. We both love you. This is the best possible solution for everybody. You know it is."

"Yeah, well, it sure is for me, I think, but what about you, my savage man. Can you do it? Can she?"

"I believe she can. In truth, I believe she wants to. Dee, I know this isn't the perfect solution, but I think it's the best all the way around for everybody."

"Right. Are you sure you're not just trying to get two girls in the bed at once?"

Dor gave a great bellowing laugh. "Now that's a sweet fantasy, but I doubt I could survive the reality. On the other hand, I'd probably die with a smile on my face."

"Fool." She laughed and poked him in the ribs again. "Talk to me, mister. I have the feeling you already have it all worked out in your head."

"Well, as I see it, Chella and I will be sharing more than a companion. We'll be sharing a ship."

"Explain."

"All right. For the sake of argument, say we all swear the bond. When the Warbird lifts off for the next mission I will be the captain and Chella will be first man on the Raptor. That will give you two a chance to re-connect. Then when the next mission comes up I get my job back and she returns to her ship."

"You've got it all worked out, haven't you? Why, Dor?"

"Because I love you madly and want you to be happy. When you're happy my world is bright. When you're unhappy, I hurt."

"So this won't hurt?"

"Not nearly as much. I mean that."

"I love you too, crazy man. So, okay, that's all fine and shiny, but what happens when all the ships are on the ground as they will be in a day or two?"

"Oh that's the best part," he replied, a twinkle in his eye. "That's when I get both girls."

Her eyes went wide and her mouth made a perfect O. "Oh you beast!" With that she pounced on him and began beating him with the pillow.

Late the next day they arrived at the hunting lodge planet. Locating a clearing near running water, they set the ships down. It was getting late so a camp was set up, but the hunters would wait until morning. Since Gold Nova was low on supplies, Red Nova hosted the feast. Deann was organizing things, so Dor wandered off towards the Warbird.

Michella was the last of her people off the ship. She looked all around and finally spotted Dor waiting for her. She went to him and linked her arm through his. For good or ill she had made her decision. This mad scheme of his could heal the wound in her life, and she was ready to take that chance. "So, where's Dee?" she asked as she gave his arm a gentle squeeze.

"Organizing as usual. Chella, it's decision time. You need this, Dee needs this, and I need it. Will you swear the bond with us?"

She had a twinkle in her eye as she responded. "Was that an official proposal, Dor?"

He gazed in her eyes for a moment and saw the merriment there. "Why, yes it was, beautiful lady."

"In that case, as crazy as it all sounds, I accept. So, just where is our third and why isn't she here?"

"She's embarrassed, Chella. She figured out what I'd done and is afraid to face you."

"She figured it out and you're still alive? Wow, she really does love you."

"I know, and I thank the stars daily for it. Chella, she's embarrassed and unsure now. Please go talk to her."

"Oh I will, sweetie, and you're coming with me. After all, this was your idea."

"Me?"

"You. You just proposed to me, and I accepted. Now we're going to tell your companion. Come on." Without further ado, with her arm still linked through his, she dragged him off to find Deann. They found her talking to Micha.

"Forgive me, Poppa, but I need this woman right now." Michella linked her free arm through Deann's and led her away to a spot out of everyone's hearing. Deann was blushing furiously and wouldn't meet her eyes.

Michella tipped Deann's chin up with gentle fingers. "Dee, this man just proposed to me and I accepted. I assumed that you're willing to share the bond, is this true?" Deann just gazed into her eyes longingly and nodded. "Was that nod an official proposal?" Again Deann nodded, more enthusiastically this time. "In that case, I accept both of you. Dor, find a priestess. Let's get this done."

Wide eyed, Dor went to find Nellie while Deann hugged Michella fiercely. He soon returned with Nellie as well as most everybody else, including Micha and Edie. Deann swallowed hard as Chella stepped between her and Dor, put her arms around them and pulled them close. "Someone wanted a priestess?" asked Nellie, a twinkle in her eyes and using her sexy purr.

Michella nodded, took a deep breath, then spoke. "Nellie, Priestess of Red Nova, this man and this woman have asked me to share their bond of companionship. I've agreed to do so. Will you witness for us?"

"Well it's about time," Nellie's voice sounded in her mind. Aloud she said, "Dor of Red Nova, is it truly your wish to share your bond to Deann with Michella of Gold Nova?"

"That is my wish, Priestess," he replied putting his arm around Michella's waist and kissing her cheek.

"Deann, Chieftain of Red Nova, is it truly your wish to share your bond of love to Dor with this woman?"

Deann took a deep breath and straightened up. When she spoke it was the chieftain speaking as well. "It is indeed my wish to live with, and express my love for, both Dor of Red Nova and Michella of Gold Nova."

"Then I declare it so. You three are now bonded to each other by sworn oath and the bonds of love. May happiness shine upon you and bless your union." A rousing cheer went up causing them all to blush.

"All right you two, it's time to take your new bride home," declared Michella, as she strode away, towing the both of her new companions along with her. There were whistles and good-natured catcalls following behind them. It wasn't until they were all in the chieftain's cabin aboard the Raptor that she lost her bravado.

They stood shyly gazing at each other for a moment then Dor stepped to Michella, smiled gently at her, then took the baby in his sling from around her neck. "Come on, Little Blue, let's you and me go do some man stuff. We'll leave these girls here so they don't mess up our mojo." He stepped through the door carrying the sleeping child. "Stop wasting time and get to know one another again," he said as he closed the door. They heard him walking away. "So, Blue, you want to go drinking with the guys?"

"Does he never stop?" asked Michella.

"Nope, so you might as well get used to it. He's a good man, Chella."

"I know, Dee. I believe you. I won't hold back from him."

"Chella?"

"Dee, I fully expected that was part of the deal. It had to be or Nellie would never have sealed it. You know that's true."

"So, you've had eyes on my guy all along?"

"Well, he is a ..." She got no further as Deann sealed her lips with a kiss.

When their passion was spent Michella pulled Deann closer. "Go to sleep, my love, my precious girl. I've missed holding you like this. Go to sleep." With a soft purr, Deann snuggled down and melted into her lover's embrace.

Michella awakened hours later with Deann still in her arms. She wept tears of joy and gently tightened the arms around her lover. Deann purred and snuggled closer. Michella fought to remain still and not disturb the girl, but her breasts were aching and she squirmed a bit to try and ease them.

"Mmm, Chella, my sweet delicious Chella," murmured Deann, as she nuzzled Michella's belly then rolled to her back and stretched. "Gods it was good to wake up in your arms again."

"I know sweetie, I know. I've dreamed of this day for months. Honey, have you any idea where Dor might be?"

"Dor?"

"He took the baby. I need ..."

"Oh yeah, you're pretty full aren't you," grinned Deann, as she gave Michella's breast a gentle squeeze. "Hang on." She groped around until she found her clothes on the floor and then the comm unit. "Chieftain to Dor of Red Nova."

"Dor here," came the response. They could hear the baby fussing in the background.

"You and Baby Blue have had enough partying for one night. Get your butt back here."

"On our way." In a few short minutes he stepped through the door and handed the baby over to his mamma. Chella swiftly got the child latched onto a breast then sighed with relief as he suckled nosily.

Deann was pulling on her clothes, tucking away her weapons when she looked up. He was watching her with a gentle smile on his face. "Dor?"

"None of that now," he said, as he pulled her close and kissed her gently. "You look more relaxed and at peace than you have in a long time, Dee. I'm truly happy for you."

"But not..."

"Hush now, look at that smile on the face of our new bride. Actually, ladies, I'm rather pleased with myself. I love it when a plan works out. Now, I'll just go check in on the bridge while you two ..."

"Belay that," grinned Deann, as she winked at Michella. "You stay right there; I'll check in with the bridge."

Wide-eyed, Dor watched her leave then turned back to Michella who was just switching the baby onto her other breast. "So, where did you spend the night?" she asked.

"I was over checking out the Warbird."

"What? Why?"

"I need to know the ship if I'm going to captain her."

"Did I miss something here?"

"Chella, when the Bird flies next I'll be on the bridge, you'll be first man here. After that mission you get your ship back and I'll be first man here."

"Oh, I see. So you've got it all worked out, have you?"

There was something about her tone that alerted him. "Chella? What did I miss?"

"Did you, or did you not, swear the bond with me?"

"Yes I did, but..."

"Then why the hell are you trying to get away from me?"

"What? Chella, I don't understand ..."

"As your bonded companion, I fully expect to share your bed."

"Hey now, relax, there's no ..."

"Don't you find me attractive?"

"What? Good gods yes, but ..."

"Then what? Don't you want me?"

"You're scaring me, woman."

"Answer the question, tell me the truth, do you, or do you not, want me?"

"Oh lord, girl, want you? Dee would shoot me for what I'm thinking. Chella, you don't have to push yourself here."

She laid the now sleeping child on a bundle of clothes on the floor and tucked him in. Dor was painfully aware that she was still naked. She straightened up then stepped into his arms and kissed him, her hand sliding into his uniform and grasping his rising member. Her eyes opened wide as she felt him twitch and grow in her hand. "Oh my, well, at least he finds me attractive." She pulled his head down and kissed him deeply.

A short while later she lay in his arms, listening to him breathe. "There now," she said. "That wasn't so bad, was it?"

He laughed and hugged her tightly. "You're a crazy woman. Chella, there was no need ..."

"Hush, Dor. For me, this was implied from the start. A three way bond has to be a fully loving three way bond."

"That's what held you back? Why you wanted to talk to me on the Warbird before making a final decision? The idea of me and you ..."

"Do you know what happened to me? How little Michan came to be?"

"I do."

"So you fully expected I wouldn't want your touch. I understand now. Dor, I have no problems here, nor does Dee. We three will share the cabin. Someone else will fly the Warbird. You and I will take time to grow closer, we three will find a way to make it all work."

"We could bring her into the Red fleet then you and I could take turns."

"Let's worry about that later. Right now we should go make sure Dee hasn't started another war somewhere."

Trial by Combat

They found Deann outside getting ready to enjoy her morning meal. All the children and warriors had already eaten, and the hunting parties were ready to leave.

Deann looked them both in the eye and they blushed. Dor watched her carefully for any sign of jealousy but saw none. All he saw was the tiny smile playing at her lips. "Didn't count on that when you made all these fancy plans, did you?"

Dor blushed to his roots then turned towards the departing hunters. "Alise," he shouted. "Don't you even think about leaving me behind."

"I would never consider such a thing. Hurry." She was grinning and so was everyone else. Dor kissed the girls on the cheek, caught the bow Alise tossed to him, and trotted away with the others.

"He hunts with a bow?" asked Michella.

"Alise taught him how to make and use them," replied Deann. "On the time ship ammo had to be saved for the enemy. Before that he used a spear."

"There's more to the man than I realized."

"Starting to grow on you, is he?"

Michella smiled. "Yeah, he is."

"Alas, poor Dor."

"What's that supposed to mean?"

"He had it all worked out, Chella, in his mind. We'd swear the three way bond, I'd be happy, you'd be happy, and he could live with it. In his plan you and he would trade off flying the Warbird and I'd always have one of you with me."

"So, I ask again, why poor Dor?"

Deann gave a delighted laugh. "The one thing he couldn't account for in his plan, and I doubt it crossed his mind, really, was you."

"Me?"

"Dor thinks of me as the ultimate take charge woman. He had no way to calculate your true response to the whole plan."

"But you did?"

"I know you, Chella. You could see that I love him, so I knew you'd go the distance to love him too. Otherwise, it would all be a lie and you'd never be able to live with that."

"You're right there, Dee, but of course, he couldn't know that."

"So, did you scare him to death?"

Michella laughed at that. "Oh gods, Dee, yes I did. I asked him if he found me attractive. He said you'd shoot him for what he was thinking. Poor boy looked terrified."

Now Deann was laughing. She stopped and gazed lovingly at Michella. "Sweetheart, are you all right? I mean. ..."

"I'm fine, Dee. It was strange, both with his touch and his, you know, but it wasn't what I expected."

"Oh?"

"Actually I was terrified I'd panic when he touched me, but he was so gentle. It was like he was making me lead all the way."

"Now that's my Dor. Once you're comfortable with him he'll loosen up a bit, but until he's sure he'll baby you all the way."

"All things considered, that's not such a bad thing."

"I'm glad you're okay, my love. I can't begin to express how relieved I am that ... oh skeeter, here comes Micha and he doesn't look happy."

They waited a moment until he joined them. "What's up, Poppa?"

"Girls, we've got problems. I just got a message; Kella's inbound with news. Good news comes in messages, bad news comes in person."

"How much time have we got?" asked Deann.

"Kella will arrive by nightfall. I'm sorry you two, three, don't have more time to ..."

"Hey, It's all right, Poppa. However, you'll need a new captain for the Warbird. Old Rath or Hawk would be my choice."

"And you'd be mine, Chella, but we'll sort that out later. Right now we have to top up our supplies then head for the king's lodge where he's made a fuel dump for us. We can fuel up all our ships there."

"All right," said Deann, "then we have to deal with Kemge and Goro right now. I'm not flying my ship into battle with those two on board."

"Never leave a live enemy at your back?" grinned Micha.

"Exactly, so what do you want to do with them?"

"Call the people together," replied Micha. "We'll get this done while the hunters are out." He turned and walked back towards the main camp.

Deann started giving orders. "Chella, fetch your people." She reached for the comm unit at her shoulder. "Chieftain to Girta."

"Girta here."

"Call the clan together with Gold Nova."

"Understood."

"Chieftain to Linee."

"Here, Chieftain."

"Linee, bring your prisoners out to the gathering. If either of them tries anything, kill him."

"Understood, Chieftain."

The clan gathered and Linee came out of the Raptor with both her prisoners marching ahead of her. "Make a circle," said Micha. "Give us room. Bring me Kemge." Linee pushed Kemge into the open circle where Micha was waiting.

"What sort of a farce is this?" asked Kemge, a sneer on his face.

"This is your trial," replied Micha.

"Oh really? And who is to be the judge? The Black Witch?"

"Fate," said Micha. "I warned you what would happen if you came at me again. This is a trial by combat. If you win, you go free." Kemge swallowed hard as Micha stuck a huge knife in the ground then backed away so they were equal distances from it.

"Wait," came a voice that started out deep, but cracked and climbed into a higher register. "He's mine." The boy who stepped out was about thirteen years old, a bit taller than Micha, but there was no mistaking who he was.

"No, son," Micha said kindly, "you're too young yet."

"I'm not, Father. I've already killed two men in battle when I was ten. This piece of misery is the man who started it all. Because of him they took me, broke my ribs, beat me, and left me tied up in my own skeet. I want him, it's payback time."

"Kon ..."

"Look out!" Kon had seen Kemge go for the knife. He pushed his father out of the way then grabbed Kemge's wrist and threw him. Kenge rolled to his feet and it was the boy facing him. "Come on. Come and get it, you sniveling coward. I'm just a boy, a child, surely you can defeat me." Kemge lunged at him, but Kon easily rolled away, coming back to his feet facing the man.

Terrified for his son, Micha none the less stayed his hand. Old Rath held him back. "Let the boy work, Micha," he said softly. "Let him work."

The old man was grinning and Micha suddenly realized the old assassin had been teaching Kon as he had Deann. He turned back to the combatants in time to see Kon duck beneath another wild lunge and deliver a crushing kick to Kemge's knee. As the much larger man struggled back to his feet, favoring the crippled knee, Old Rath shouted. "Kon. Number seven."

The boy never took his eyes off his enemy, but he gave a curt nod. He began to circle Kemge slowly, forcing the man to turn onto the injured leg to face him. When Kemge finally made a desperate lunge Kon leaped in, seized the man's wrist as his body turned. Kemge was thrown to the ground where he landed heavily. Suddenly realizing his weapon was gone, he struggled back to his feet. The knife was in Kon's hand.

His eyes went wide as the boy slid the dagger into his boot. "They beat me, kicked me, and threw me around. Now it's payback time. Defend yourself." He came in fast and delivered a smashing blow to Kemge's ribs, but the big man managed to grab hold of his tunic. Kon was spun through the air by the sudden jerk on his clothes.

Edie gasped from the sidelines as Kemge swung his huge foot, but Kon, now on his back, spun away then spun back again to deliver another crushing kick to the side of the man's good knee. With a howl of pain, Kemge fell headlong. He tried to right himself, but the boy was on his back, powerful legs wrapped around his chest squeezing the air from his lungs. Strong arms, far too strong for a normal boy of thirteen, encircled his neck and tightened.

Kemge flopped over rolling onto the boy, but Kon didn't relent; he just tightened his holds. Slowly but surely the fight went out of the big man and he went limp. The boy didn't relax his grip, he just squeezed harder. Finally it was Micha gently tugging at him that brought Kon back to reality. "Easy now, son, easy. He's dead. Easy now, let go now and I'll help you up."

Kon finally relaxed his hold then allowed his father to help him to stand. He was trembling and didn't trust his voice. Old Rath stepped up and nudged the body with the toe of his boot. "Your form was a bit sloppy on that number seven," he said.

Shocked, Kon met his eyes then noticed the merriment there. The old fellow's grin broke wide and Kon laughed. "Kon boy, come with me, we'll get something to eat then practice that number seven some more."

Micha watched them go then turned to see Deann looking at him. "What?"

"Where do you want this one?"

"Him? He's your problem." He was astonished at how fast it happened. The words were barely past his lips when her arm flashed out and Goro's eyes rolled back in his head, trying to see the knife that was buried in his skull. Micha nodded in admiration of the power of that throw. It takes a lot of force to penetrate a skull.

As the body sank to the ground Deann called for Quint. "Aye, Chieftain."

"Get a couple of men to carry those bodies back into the woods a way. Don't bother to bury them, just get them out of sight."

"Understood." He pointed to a couple of men and they stepped out, gathered up the bodies, and followed him away from the encampment.

"That was a little cold, Dee."

"Sorry, Chella. Sometimes I think I lost my humanity back on that ship years ago."

"I'll do what I can to help you find it again. I promise." Deann just smiled and reached for her hand. "I'll let Hawk know there's no need for the king to waste time sending a prisoner pick up. Tell me, if there'd been time to wait for one, would you have?"

"Yeah, I would. However, I don't think there's going to be a lot of time. If Kella's news is as bad as your father thinks it will be, I expect to be back in space before morning. I won't go into battle with a scheming enemy at my back."

"Those were hard years, weren't they Dee."

"Yeah, they were. I spent a lot of time fighting and a lot of time studying."

"Studying?"

"The history of Red Nova. I needed to know where I went wrong last time. I looked for the weaknesses that grew over time, the mistakes in battle plans, etc. Chella, just between you and me, by the time the iron emperor reached Nova's borders he should have been weakened.

The Borelian Clans wouldn't go down easy, and I've fought his forces. I know some of their tactics."

"Are you saying Red Nova should have been able to defeat him?"

"Yeah, I think they should have. There was no lack of courage there, but a few practices down through the generations made his victory possible."

"And one of those was taking prisoners."

"Yes, take prisoners and you have to feed them, watch them. That's a big drain on your resources. Another problem was the loss of the witches. I have to talk to Lady Arlessa about that. Then there was the lack of education and training."

"Okay, I can see where your focus is here. How can I help?"

"Just help old Dor keep me sane."

"I will, sweetie. I will."

The day passed in preparations for war. Deann believed in being ready for the worst, anything better is a bonus. The hunters called in late afternoon. They needed help to get all the meat back to the ships. It was just beginning to roast on the spits when Kella's speeder arrived. After she had eaten, Micha called Deann and her captains over to hear the news.

Kella sighed and began. "Well, thanks to your warning about the impending attack and the source of the trouble, I was able to figure out who the spies were. I turned them over to the Viceroy. Lady Marla had no trouble getting them to talk.

"Here's where it stands. The RIM company has been informed that the assassination of King Borad and the capture of his kingdom was successful. That was their cue to advance their forces into Sector Nine."

"But it failed," said Deann.

"Yes, but those messages were sent before you arrived and messed up their plans. If you hadn't, it would have succeeded," replied Kella. "Now, here's the thing. At the spies best guess, RIM has already begun amassing it's forces. They'll be moving towards the Gap as we speak."

"Skeet," muttered Micha.

"What are their numbers?" asked Deann. "What are the abilities of their ships, how many do they have, which pathway through the Gap will they use?"

Arlessa grinned and gently poked Micha in the ribs. He smiled and sat back. Kella saw the shift, and without missing a beat, turned her attention to Deann. "At best guess they'll mount about a thousand ships. The capabilities of those ships will be about the same as the one you gave Zemma a while back. The real bad news is, they're coming through the Gap in all three pathways. They want to be spread out to hit as many targets as possible when they arrive. The idea is to crush Arcalia between them and Sega Clan."

Deann frowned and stared at the fire for a while. No one spoke to disturb her. Finally she spoke. "Micha? What do you want to do here?"

"Me? I want to retire and go back to farming while I'm still young enough to wield a hoe. I hereby resign as chieftain of Nova Clan and appoint Deann of Red Nova as grand Chieftain."

"Denied," she grinned at him. "What's your second option?" There was a great round of laughter at that.

"All right," said Micha. "One option is to stay right where we are until it's over. They're expecting a fragmented and embattled sector. They'll be met by the Viceroy's armada backed up by the Borelian Clans. They'll get their buttocks handed to them and that'll be that."

Deann just grinned at him. "I get the impression you don't like that option."

"I don't. This is the Gap, our territory. If we let them just walk through then we lose all credibility, all the respect we've tried so hard to establish. We'd have to start over from scratch. However, I'm loathe to risk all our people against such a huge force."

Deann stood up. "How about it, Red Nova? Are you willing to risk battle against a much larger force deep in the Gap?" The roar of Aye!

was nearly deafening. "Gold Nova?" Another Aye! She sat back down. "All Nova is ready to defend our territory. How do we do it?"

"You tell me." He was grinning at her now, but she didn't seem to notice. Dor saw the shift in her and moved closer, lightly touching Michella on the arm. She met his eyes then looked closer at Deann as he indicated. She nodded and they both moved closer.

"If they're already on the move, we're out of time," said Deann. "We'll need to face them inside the Gap. Micha, you've been patrolling the first pathway. You know it and its dangers well. Can you defend it with two ships?"

"They can only come at me two to three at a time, so, yes, I can. I've got Lady Arlessa with me if it gets tight ..."

"All right, the first pathway is yours. The Dragon will accompany you. She's faster and more agile than the Ravage, but you know the area. Girta, will fly with you under your command."

"Works for me," said Girta. "I can upgrade my ship's maps at the same time."

"Zartah, you know the ways and dangers of the second pathway."

"I do. It's a bit wider than the first one, but has a number of nasty surprises."

Deann thought for a moment then sighed. "All right, Zartah, the second route is yours. The Comet and the Raptor will fly with you."

She turned to Michella, her jaw set. Michella gave her a smile, her eyes dancing. "I'll take the Warbird and defend the third route, Dee. Nobody knows that route like we do, you know that. It's changed a lot since we took over and it's a tight squeeze in lots of places. I can defend it."

"Want a faster ship?"

"No, I want the ship I know, the crew I know. I know exactly what the Bird can and will do in there. There's no time to get used to a new ship."

"Gods, I hate to send you in alone."

"Send me," said Dor. "It's my turn to fly the Bird anyway."

"Forget that, sweetheart," said Michella. "You and your woman may have stolen my heart, but you're not stealing my ship." That brought another round of laughter. She reached to give both Deann and Dor a gentle squeeze. "I'll be fine. Trust me."

Deann nodded then spoke to the gathering again. "Are there any other options?" No one spoke. "Opinions?" Again, no answer. "All right then. At first light we stock up the ships, go to top up the fuel, then we head for our assigned pathways at best speed. Everybody meet back here when it's over. Fly true, my brothers and sisters, fight hard and fly true."

The gathering broke up after that and Deann sought her cabin. Michella was right on her arm. When they entered they found Dor with a small pack on his way out. "Where are you going?" asked Michella.

"Thought I'd go camp out on the Warbird tonight."

"What? Why? You belong here with us."

Dor gently hugged her. "Listen to me now, my beautiful bride. You too, my Chieftain. In the morning we'll be flying out in different directions. Take this night for yourselves."

"Dor, no," said Michella. "I don't want that."

"Neither do I," added Deann.

"Yes you do, and you both know it. Listen to me now, my loves. Take this last night before we all fly out. It'll be a long time before we reunite, if we ever do. Take this time to make up for some of the time you've lost."

"If we ever do?" asked Michella. "Listen you, I've told you before, you're not getting out of this marriage now. I'll do this, just this one time only, if you swear you will never again try to play the martyr for me. You hear me, Dor of Red Nova?"

"I swear it to you, Chella. Never again." He kissed her lightly then kissed Deann. "I love you," he whispered, then stepped out the door.

War in the Gap

The next morning Michella awakened with Deann in her arms and she wept for joy again. Deann purred and snuggled closer where she was held tightly. A moment later, the morning klaxon sounded and she opened her eyes then kissed Michella before hopping out of bed. Deann dressed swiftly then grabbed her comm unit. "Deann to Dor. Get your butt over to the Warbird and say your goodbyes. We need to get in the air."

"Acknowledged."

Michella was trying to pull her clothes on while nursing the baby. Deann helped her then kissed her deeply. "I love you madly and Dor loves you too. Fight hard, my love. Come back to us."

"I will, Dee, I promise."

Deann handed her an info stick. "Take this. Broadcast it to Zemma and she'll back you up."

"You sure about that?"

"She will or I'll have her hide." With that and another kiss, Deann fled the cabin and headed for the bridge.

Michella put the baby in the sling then hurried off to her own ship. Dor was waiting for her at the ramp. She threw herself into his arms and hugged him tightly. "Don't you ever do that to me again, Dor or I'll start thinking you don't want me."

"Stop it, woman. I do the teasing, remember? Chella, fight hard, but be careful. Come back to us."

"Us?"

"Us, and to me, dammit woman I wasn't expecting to fall for you so fast and hard. You bring yourself back, do you hear?"

For an answer she kissed him deeply, holding it until he pulled her tight to him and moaned. As their lips parted she gently pushed him back. "That'll have to hold the both of us until we get back." He hugged her tightly again then reluctantly let her go.

Dor ran to the Raptor and hurried to the bridge. "You okay?" asked Deann.

"As good as can be under the circumstances."

"Didn't count on that, did you?"

"Count on what?"

"Chella as a person in her own right. She's a real force of nature and easy to love, isn't she?"

"She sure is. Easy to see why you couldn't forget her, Dee."

"Okay, are we ready?"

"Ready."

Comms, ship wide."

"Ship wide, aye," said Tanie.

"Attention people. The Raptor is about to lift off. Is everybody aboard?"

"All aboard and we're locked down, Chieftain," came Eddan's voice.

"Barah, take us to orbit."

"Orbit, Aye."

The ship rose gracefully followed by the rest. Once all ships were in orbit Deann called for ship to ship comms. "Kella, you there?"

"Here, Deann."

"I need you to take messages to the Viceroy, the king, and anybody else who is headed this way. Tell them to stay out of the Gap. There's no room in there for large numbers of ships. We'll thin them out as best we can, stall them as long as we can, then we'll withdraw and let them through. The Viceroy can have whatever is left by then."

"Understood. On my way."

"Micha, Chella, did you hear that?" asked Deann.

"Acknowledged and understood," replied Micha."

"Understood," said Michella.

"Then off we go. Zartah, take the lead. Once we reach the Gap, find us a choke point as deep in as we can get."

"Understood."

The Shield leaped away, followed closely by the Raptor and the Comet. Their pathway was the closest and they would reach it long before any of the others reached theirs. When they were two days into the Gap, Zartah called a halt then contacted Deann on a secure channel.

"What's wrong, Zartah?"

"Deann, you know we'll be facing hundreds of ships in here."

"I know."

"Okay, here's the problem. I once ran my own crew. That ended with me in prison where Micha found me. Deann, since I met Micha I've learned to know my own limitations and to know when to step aside and let someone else take the lead. That time is now."

"Zartah, you know this lane better than anybody else. I don't."

"I know, so here's my plan. I put my first man in the chair, and I come aboard the Raptor as guide. I can tell you where the pitfalls are, and you can direct the battle. You're a better leader than I am, Deann. We both know that. I love this ship and every person aboard her. I want them all to survive. I believe they stand a much better chance of that if you lead the fleet."

Deann sighed and thought for a moment. "Understood. Come on aboard. I'll inform the fleet."

"On my way."

She returned to the bridge. "Dor, Zartah is coming over to be our guide. Go meet him and bring him to the bridge."

"Aye, Chieftain. What should I do with the stowaway?"

"Stowaway? What stowaway?"

"Micha's son, Kon."

"What??? Where was he hiding?"

"In the brig. Apparently, Linee's taken a shine to him."

"Are you kidding me? Micha will skin me alive. Dammit anyway. Put both of them in the brig. I'll deal with them in a while." Grinning, Dor left the bridge. Everybody else studied their panels and avoided her eyes. Nobody envied those two youngsters.

Dor returned with Zartah who gave her a nod of thanks. "People, this man is Zartah, our guide. If he gives an order, obey it. Dor, take the chair. Get this fleet moving again." Dor settled into the chair and she left he bridge.

Zartah looked confused so Barah took pity on him. "We have a stowaway on board, Dad. Kon is here and Dee is on her way to get him."

"Kon? Skeet, Micha and Edie will be frantic. Can we get a message to them?"

"Nope," said Dor. "We'll have to work that out later, if he survives. The chieftain didn't look happy. All right, Zartah, talk to our pilot. Let's get under way."

Deann stalked into the brig to find both youngsters in adjoining cells. "Stand up." They rose to their feet, not meeting her eyes. She stepped up to Kon's cell. "Look me in the eye." He raised his head. "Does your father know you're here?"

"By now he probably does. I told Odea where I was going, but told her to say nothing until it was too late."

Deann turned to Linee. "Did you know about this."

"No, she didn't," said Kon.

"Did I speak to you? No. Linee, answer me."

"No, Chieftain. I didn't."

"Tell me."

"We were two days out when I found him. Actually, I heard him snoring," she giggled.

"But you still didn't tell me ..., you told Dor, didn't you."

"Yes, Chieftain. He said to feed him and keep him out of sight for a few more days."

Deann sighed. "All right, Linee, come out of there."

The girl grinned as she swung the cell door open and stepped out. "How did you know it wasn't locked?"

"The keys are still on your belt, besides, I know Dor." She tuned back to Kon. "How old are you?"

"Thirteen, almost fourteen."

"Right, almost fourteen. Why did you do this?"

"I want to fight. Poppa will have me in the nursery with the other babies. I'm a man now. I've killed men in battle, and I have the right to fight for Nova."

"Why my ship?"

"It was the closest."

"Lie to me again and you'll never get out of there."

His shoulders sagged and his face turned bright red. "Because Linee's on this ship."

Deann groaned. "Do you have any idea what you've done? No, you don't. Let me explain. I find you on my ship and turn back to chase after Micha. I find him back at the hunting grounds, his whole crew searching the forest for you. By then Company forces have poured through both alleyways through the Gap. We're caught on the ground and there are no Nova survivors except those on Chella's ship."

The boy swallowed hard, and he looked close to tears. Deann didn't relent. "I won't stop and turn back and hopefully Micha won't either. What you did was beyond stupid. You want to fight? You want to be part of this battle?

"Let me tell you something you should already know, mister. This isn't hand-to-hand on the ground, this is a battle in the air, ship against ship. Do you know who fights a battle like that? People, and a human in a good ship is as good as a Novan in a good ship. People who obey orders the instant they're uttered. They don't argue, they don't hesitate, and they never talk back. That's how you fight a battle like this." He didn't respond, but he was shaking. She finally relented.

"When was the last time you had a meal?"

"Before we lifted off. Linee brought me some food, but ..."

"Can you operate ships comms?"

"What? Yes, of course I can."

"Then you're my new comms officer. Let me tell you this, hesitate or disobey me even once and it won't be Kemge you face in battle, it'll be me, and I'll take the hide off you. Linee."

"Here, Chieftain."

"Take him up to the mess and feed him, find him quarters, then send him to the bridge. If you two let your hormones get the better of your judgment again, I'll shoot the pair of you." With that she stalked out and returned to the bridge.

Dor moved out of the chair, and she slid into place. "Talk to me, Dor."

"I knew you wouldn't turn back, but I wanted him to have a few more days to think about what you might do to him. He said he left word with a friend."

"So we're doing good guy, bad guy now, are we?"

"Don't we always?"

"Remind me to shoot you later."

"Yes, Chieftain. So, is he still in the brig?"

"Linee's feeding him then he'll be here on the bridge where we can keep him out of trouble."

"The bridge, in a battle?" asked Zartah.

"On comms," replied Deann. "Once it goes crazy he'll feel safer with people he knows around him, you, Nellie, Barah and me. It'll be easier for him to hold it together."

Zartah smiled and nodded. "Knew I made the right choice," he said.

"Oh yeah, so where are we?" she asked.

"We're about three days from where I'd like to be. We're passing through a wide spot right now, but it's quite narrow behind us. If we have to run we might be able to scrub off a few back there."

"Okay, so what's up ahead that you like so much?"

"A pair of anomalies appeared last year. I doubt if anybody on the other side is aware of them yet. They narrow the passageway a bit, but the best part for us is when one of their ships hit one of them. You hit one and your ship is thrown back, spinning like crazy. Everybody on board lost their lunch when that happened to us. Even the inertial dampeners couldn't keep up to it. Imagine if one of them hit it and the rest were tight behind."

Deann had a wolfish grin on her face. "Loving that one. What else have we got?"

"Well, just in past it is a wide stretch. Lots of room, but you come into it through a narrow area. That part has been pretty stable for a long time."

"All right, that's where we'll set up. Can we hide just inside the wide area."

"Hide?"

"Two ships, one on each side, out of sight. Here's the idea, We confront them, they bluster and attack. We can outfight a good number of them, draw them into the trap. We'll finish a bunch of them that way, but they'll eventually push us back by sheer force of numbers. We run for it, duck between the anomalies then turn to fight again. That'll cause them to fan out to attack us."

Zartah grinned. "That'll drive a lot of them into the anomalies."

"Right. We fight whoever makes it through that, and then we fall back to the next narrow spot when we have to. If enough of them make it through that, we run for it and let the viceroy deal with whatever is left. Is there anything useful further on?"

"Not really," replied Zartah. "The best they can do is get five ships wide in a formation anywhere in the Gap. These are the choke points."

"All right, we're in place. All we can do now is wait. Zartah, I have the placements now, if you want to return to the Shield."

"I can stay if you want. Gorda's in the chair over there."

"Lady Norlene with you, too?"

"Yep, she is."

"Good to know," said Deann. "Barah, have you got the exact coordinates of all the important stuff?"

"The good and the bad, aye Chieftain."

"Transmit that to the Comet."

"Transmitting now, Chieftain."

"Okay, we're good then. Go home now, Zartah. Go back and tell Miriam how proud she should be of Barah. He's the best pilot there is, and he'll remember every coordinate. You can trust that. I have everything I need."

Zartah gazed at his blushing son for a moment then smiled with a father's pride. He nodded then turned towards the door. "Deann, the Shield will be ready." She smiled and patted his arm as he left.

She heard him speak again just outside the door to the bridge. "You're in a heap of skeet, boy, once your father gets his hands on you."

A moment later Kon entered the bridge. "Kon of Nova reporting for duty, Chieftain."

Deann didn't even look at him. "You're on comms." Nellie slid out of the way to let him take the chair. She patted his shoulder and gave him a reassuring smile as he took his station.

Once Zartah was aboard the Shield again, Deann spoke. "Comms, ship-to-ship."

"Ship-to-ship, aye. Go ahead, Captain."

"That's Chieftain to you, mister," said Dor as he winked at Kon. "Never forget who you're talking to."

"Comet, Shield, this is the Raptor. We seem to have arrived early for the party. Quint, have you got the battle coordinates yet?"

"Received and installed, Chieftain."

"All right, people. Since we're here, we might as well have a few practice runs. Quint, to the left, find a hiding spot. Zartah, to the right. We'll just hang out here as bait." And so the drills began. For eight days they practiced their tactics until Deann's sensors picked up ships incoming.

The clang of the klaxon rang throughout the ship and brought Deann from a sound sleep. "Battle stations, battle stations, Chieftain to the bridge. We have incoming."

Deann came pounding onto the bridge and threw herself into the chair. "Tanie, how many?"

"Too many to count, Chieftain," replied Tanie. "That's the right party all right. They're flying three abreast and there no end in sight of the convoy."

"Comms."

"Comms, aye."

It was Kon and the look of anticipation on his face told her he was ready. She nodded approvingly. "Hail them."

"Channel open, Chieftain."

"Attention oncoming ships. You're encroaching on Nova Clan territory. Power down and identify or be destroyed."

"And just who are you, my beauty, who will destroy five hundred warships with your single ship?"

"This is Deann of Red Nova aboard the Raptor. Last chance, power down and identify or be destroyed."

The big man in the fancy uniform who appeared on the screen was grinning with delight. "This is Admiral Exton aboard the flagship Terra New. Lock up with me and we'll discuss your surrender over a hot meal." He did not get the answer he expected.

"So be it. Helm, attack speed." She jerked her hand and Kon cut the connection. The Raptor leaped forward, firing as she went. The mighty flagship tried to evade and return fire, but it was slow and clumsy compared to the Raptor. The ship exploded as did the three closest to it. The Raptor made a tight turn that shouldn't have been possible and attacked the next three ships. Two went down, then she took several direct hits.

The shielding held, but she made a run for it. The RIM ships gave chase, but were suddenly caught in the crossfire. No one in the company fleet had ever seen ships that could move and fight at that speed before. Several more went down, but they kept coming. The available space for maneuvering was swiftly filling up.

"Dee, we're running out of room," said Barah.

"Comms, ship-to-ship."

"Ship-to-ship, aye. Go ahead, Chieftain." replied Kon.

"Quint, Zartah, fall back." As practiced, both ships turned and ran. They soon disappeared behind an anomaly. "Helm, full astern. Gunners, keep them busy." The Raptor was doing a merry dance to avoid the almost solid wall of enemy fire. She took a number of hits, then turned and ran.

They blasted past the two anomalies and turned to fight. Suddenly three of the pursuing ships were hurled spinning into the mass of ships behind them. Ships were exploding and others trying to avoid collisions. Several of those hit the anomaly and met the same fate. The Raptor just sat waiting.

It took hours and only two ships made it through. The Raptor shot them down. And again she waited. Dor spoke up at last. "Dee, you've been on the bridge for over twelve hours now. You need to rest."

"So do you."

"You first."

"Sensors, anything moving over there?"

"Negative, Chieftain. There're too many derelicts in the way; they can't get through."

"Comms, ship to ship, secure channels."

"Ship-to-ship, secure channels, aye." The boy sounded tired, but he was still there. Deann smiled and gave him an approving nod.

"Zartah, How's the Shield holding up?"

"Ship is sound, Chieftain. Crew is a bit tired."

"Quint, how's the Comet?"

"She's sound and battle ready, Chieftain. Crew is a bit weary."

"Understood. Put on minimal crews with double attention to sensors. At the first sign of trouble run for it. Get some rest people. Dor, get me a few fresh faces up here then everybody get some sleep."

Her tired crew left the bridge as three new people arrived. They looked to be much more rested. One of them was Ordoo, an Eldin. "I have a good memory, Chieftain. I have studied the coordinates of this pathway. I can watch the sensors and pilot the ship to an escape."

Deann nodded. Linee came and took the gunner's chair while Tanie, who had been sent for a rest earlier returned and took the chair. Deann sighed deeply then retreated to her cabin. Dor joined her a few minutes later, but she was already asleep. He grinned and cuddled her close.

Many hours later, they arrived in the mess for a meal. Most of the bridge crew were there already. They chatted easily among themselves for a while, enjoyed the meal, then headed for the bridge to relieve the night crew. Deann and Dor soon joined them. "Report," said Deann, as she eased into the captain's chair.

"Sensors here, Chieftain. There's some movement in there, but nothing is in a hurry to come through and face the Raptor."

"Now that's good news. Dor, find out how our munitions are holding out."

"We're down to just below half, Chieftain. We've got maybe one more good fight in us then we'll have to run."

"Understood. Comms, ship-to-ship, secure channel."

"Ship-to-ship, secure channels, aye. Go ahead, Chieftain." Deann grinned. Kon looked rested and ready for another fight.

"Raptor to Shield. Anybody awake over there?"

"Barely," came Zartah's voice. "Shield is secure and in position, Chieftain. The crew is well rested, but we're down to about half on the munitions."

"Understood. Comet?"

"Quint here, Chieftain. We're still in one piece, rested, and just below half on munitions."

"Understood. Now, let's see if we can start a fight. Comms, hail the RIM ships for me."

"Hailing RIM, aye," grinned the boy. "Go ahead, Chieftain."

"This is the Raptor, Deann of Red Nova commanding. Is there anybody alive over there?"

"What do you want?" asked a tired voice. Whoever it was sounded defeated.

"What do I want? I want your useless butts out of my territory, that's what I want. If you refuse I want you dead, and I will make that happen."

"It won't help you, woman. There are hundreds more ships already through your precious Gap."

"Actually, there aren't," said Deann. "You see, we knew you were coming. We knew you were taking all three routes through the Gap, and we sent ships to patrol each pathway. I can assure you the others fared no better than you did. You see, the man who defeated the emperor himself and created the Gap is leading the defense of the other main pathway, and our best ship is defending the third and most dangerous pathway.

"So tell me, who's in charge over there now. Have you got another admiral for me to shoot?"

"I'm Captain Aelgor of the Intruder. I'm the one in command now. What do you want?"

"I already told you. So, you came at me with five hundred ships. How many have you got left?" There was no response. "Well?"

"Less than half. I don't even know what the nine hells happened back there, but when it did a number of captains panicked and tried to turn back."

"I'll bet that wasn't helpful. Listen, Aelgor, you sound like a reasonable man. Let me point out your options for you. Option one, you can blast the debris out of the way and come at me again. Do that and I'll shoot you down along with a few dozen of your compatriots. Then I'll run for it and another ship like this one with a fresh crew and a full load of munitions will take my place. The Gap has lots of interesting things for you to discover between here and Sector Nine space."

The man on the screen sighed deeply. "Are there other options?"

"Only one I can see."

"Turn back."

"That would be the one," said Deann. "It just might make you the hero of this misadventure."

"Oh?"

"The company you work for is about to lose over a thousand ships. As I said, Micha and his witches are defending the other approach. I wouldn't give a lot for those ships' chances. If you return with a few resources still functional ... well, you get the idea."

"I think you're just telling me this to avoid a fight. I think you're about out of munitions and are putting up a bold front."

Deann's eyes went hard. "You're right, Aelgor. I'm down to half munitions and so are the rest of my ships. Considering yesterday's tally that should be just about enough to finish you. Maybe you can force your way through, but you'll arrive in Arcalian space with a dozen ships, facing a very angry King Borad. Oh yes, the plot to kill him failed. He's not happy with RIM right now.

"I'm getting tired of this, Aelgor. Will you go back and save your people, or will you come at me and have all those thousands of live lost on your conscience? What'll it be?"

"I think we have a standoff, woman, that's what I think."

"Cut the comms." Kon nodded and she sighed. "Nellie, do you think you can do the witchfire thing?"

"You mean through the guns?"

"Yup."

"Sure, I think I can. What do you want me to do?"

"Take a look at the sensors until you find a ship moving around over there under its own power. Once you do, target the damn thing and roast it."

"All right, Dee, but I warn you, it'll take the good out of me. I won't be a lot of use to you after that."

"Don't risk yourself, Nellie. If it's a bad idea you can say so."

Nellie laughed. "Oh no, it's a great idea, but I'll have to sleep for a day or two afterwards."

"In that case, have at it."

Nellie studied the sensors for several minutes then returned to the forward gun station. She began to chant softly and they all felt the crackle of energy that gathered around her. Suddenly her eyes opened wide and glared at the panel, black flames dancing all around her. She slammed her hand down on the firing switch. Red flame lanced out from the firing port and straight into the mess before them. It cut through two derelicts, hit the ship beside Aelgor's, sliced through that and the one behind it.

Deann caught Nellie as she practically melted out of her seat. "Barah, take her to her bed then get you buttocks back here as fast as you can. Nellie, you're the best. You're awesome. Comms, ship-to-ship."

"Ship-to-ship, aye."

Nellie grinned as she stopped to listen for a moment at the door. "Aelgor, this is Deann. You still there?"

The man came back on screen, visibly shaken. "What the hell was that?"

"That, my friend, was witchfire. Nellie, the Red Witch of Nova is unhappy with you. She has children to go home to and she's getting impatient. I don't know how much longer I can hold her in check. That was just a warning shot. If she commands me to go at you, she'll be the weapon you face. I don't recommend it."

He visibly slumped, defeated and broken. "All right, you win. I'll take what's left of our ships and return to company headquarters."

"Aelgor, tell them the Gap is ours and we will defend it. Nova Clan patrols the Gap and this is what you faced, a Novan patrol. Tell the company. You come into Nova territory with ill intent, you don't go home. Next time I won't offer that option."

"Understood."

"Go home, Aelgor. Go home to your family."

She motioned for Kon to cut the connection then returned to her chair. Barah was already back at pilot. "Nellie okay, Barah?"

"She's sleeping, Dee. She'll be fine in a day or two."

"We're being hailed by the Shield, Chieftain."

"On screen."

It was Norlene. "Deann, is Nellie all right?"

"I believe so, Lady. She'll have to sleep it off for a day or two, but I'll ask Leen to look in in her anyway."

"All right. If you need me to come over for a healing, just call. Oh, and you can tell her from me, that was one impressive display. I was years practicing before I could do that. How long has she been working on it, do you know?"

"Far as I know that was her first attempt."

Norlene paused for a moment. "I see. Deann, be careful not to make her angry."

"Understood," replied Deann, smiling.

Zartah stepped in front of the screen. "Looks like they're going home, Dee. You take your ships and go see if Chella needs help. I'll follow these characters to make sure they go where they're supposed to."

"All right, Zartah. Don't take any chances. If they play dirty just turn and make a run for it."

"Understood. Oh, thank Nellie for cutting a path through all the debris, would you."

"My pleasure," replied Deann. "See you back at the hunting grounds." She turned and sank back into her chair. "Helm, take us out of here, best speed."

"Heading home, aye." The Raptor and the Comet turned and left, but the Shield remained. Aelgor's sensors registered a lone ship following as he trailed along behind the remains of the armada. Once the tally was finished only one hundred eighty-seven ships remained of the five hundred that had entered the Gap at the central point.

Three days later, the Raptor and Comet blasted out into Arcalian space to find the Borelian Clans waiting in force. "We're being hailed, Chieftain."

"On screen, Kon." The screen lit up and Deann faced a tall woman with a wild mane of iron gray hair. "This is Deann of Red Nova aboard the Raptor. You're entering Nova territory. Identify or be destroyed."

Deann was grinning and the woman let out a long howl of laughter. Finally she got her breath back and grinned at the screen. "This is Harral of Gemsa Clan, allies of Nova Clan. Don't shoot, we're here to help."

"You're a most welcome sight, Gemsa Clan," said Deann. "Here's where we stand." She gave the woman a full report.

"Deann of Red Nova, I've heard a bit about you, but it didn't do you justice. Woman, do you know what you've done here. This was a victory worthy of Micha himself. So, Kemge is dead and so is Goro. No great loss there. So, what are your orders?"

"Orders?"

The tall woman laughed. "You said it yourself, Deann. This is your territory. How can we help? What do you need?"

"I need supplies, food and munitions for both ships. Zartah is following the imperials to make sure they leave the Gap. I told him to cut and run if they tried anything, so if he comes blasting out of there with a hundred ships on his tail ..."

"We'll swat them down for you. I have six supply ships with me. Lock up and take what you need. I get the impression you're in a hurry."

"I sent Michella into the Gap alone against gods know how many ships," replied Deann. "I need to get to her as fast as I can."

"Understood. Tema, get those supply ships up here, now. Deann, King Borad and his entire fleet are waiting at the third pathway. If your ship has to make a run for it, there's help just waiting there for her."

Deann visibly relaxed. "That's good to know."

"Here's the supply ships. Lock up now and take what you need. Harral out."

The Raptor and the Comet locked onto the supply ships. There were dozens of crew members ready and willing to do the work and in a few hours they were all topped up again. "Deann calling Harral."

"Harral here, Red Nova. You all topped up?"

"Can't thank you enough for this. I'd love to stay and chat, but I have another errand."

"Understood. I'll hang around here and wait for Zartah to check in. Oh, Deann, if you ever need anything, anything at all, you have an ally in Gemsa Clan. All you have to do is ask."

"Harral? Why would you?"

"Girl, I owe Micha my life three times over just for the Battle of the Gap. He's backed off and made you grand Chieftain of Nova. That means he's put his faith in you and that's good enough for me. You're in place to keep the galaxy off my back and I'll help you all I can. Besides, I'm sticking around until I hear all the story about Red Nova firsthand. Go on now, go see to your people."

"About Micha ..."

"The Viceroy is waiting for him at the entrance to pathway one. Get going now."

"Understood and thanks." The connection broke then Harral was amazed at the speed as the Raptor and Comet set out at full burn.

For days Deann paced, and Dor wasn't much better. They finally made contact with the flank of the Arcalian fleet and were soon in touch with the king aboard his flagship. Deann gave him a full report including the death of Goro the Usurper. "Never leave a live enemy behind you, wasn't that your credo, Deann?"

"Yes, Sire. I would have given him back to you, but we had no time to wait, and I won't fly into battle with an enemy aboard."

"Understood, and know this. I bear you no ill will at all for the execution. It was well done, and I'm well rid of him. Do you need supplies?"

"No, Sire, Harral of Gemsa Clan topped us up. I just need to get in there and make sure Michella is all right."

"Then go, with my blessing, my friend. We'll just wait here, you know, in case you might need something."

"Thank you, Sire," grinned Deann. "You're the best. Barah, into the Gap, all possible speed."

"Into the Gap, aye."

The Raptor turned swiftly, then shot between the two dwarf stars that marked the entryway to the Gap. The next day they met Zemma's two big ships limping towards them. "Comms, ship-to-ship."

"Ship-to-ship, aye."

"Deann to Zemma."

The screen lit up and Zemma's old scarred face appeared. "I'm here, Deann."

"Report."

Zemma chuckled. "There's no time, the Warbird is covering our retreat, but she's taking a pounding. Get going."

"Helm, ahead full. Battle stations, battle stations." The comm connection was lost as the Raptor shot forward. Fifteen minutes later they found the time ship floating free. The Warbird was just behind her. The Warbird was slowly working her way back towards them while fighting off a half dozen ships. They had caught her in an open pocket of space.

Aboard the Warbird there was a ragged cheer as the Raptor and Comet swept by and fell upon the enemy. It took only moments and the enemy was nothing more than scrap floating slowly towards a dead planetoid.

"Raptor to Warbird."

"Warbird here, Michella of Nova commanding. Dee, you are such a welcome sight."

"Lock up with us, Chella. Dor and I want to hug you in person."

"Aye, Chieftain. Locking up. And I'll expect more than a hug. Michella out."

After an emotional reunion, the three ships hung in space, the crews on full alert, watchful. The three lovers had eventually retired to the kitchens. They chose a meal then sat close together. Finally, Deann spoke. "Chella, what happened?"

"It was exciting, Dee," replied Michella. "We reached the entrance, sent those messages for Zemma, then headed in. We reached your time ship, but it looked dead. The energy field around it was gone and it was just drifting. We ducked under it and headed for that long tight spot. They could only get at me one at a time from there. We set up and waited. Nothing much happened for a few days then it all went to hell in a hurry.

"First, the Company ships arrived. I was just taking on the first one when I got hit from behind. Dee, I've never seen ships like that. They were big, and slow, but there were seven of them. We turned to fight, but the Company ships were pouring through by the time we had them thinned out. It wasn't looking good, but then Zemma showed up with her two ships.

"Between us, we killed the alien ships and most of the Company, but by then we were low on munitions and Zemma was completely out. I told her to run and tried to keep the company off her back until I could make a break for it. It looked like we were going down when you showed up. Thanks for coming to the rescue."

"Battle stations, Battle stations, Chieftain to the bridge."

"Skeet," said Deann, as she leaped to her feet and ran. "Chella, get back to the Bird and get her out of here. You're out of ammo and we're topped up. Go."

While Michella fled to the Warbird, Deann reached the captain's chair. "Report."

"They're coming through, Chieftain. I count eight and more coming."

"Warbird is away, Chieftain."

"Attack speed." Both the Raptor and the Comet leaped forward and engaged the enemy. They knocked down the eight and managed to block the passageway with debris. "Comms, ship-to-ship."

"Ship-to-ship, aye. Go ahead, Chieftain."

"Quint, aim your sensors behind us. I don't want any Tangles sneaking up on me."

"Understood, Chieftain."

"Attention RIM ships. You've encroached on Nova Clan territory. Power down and identify."

"This is Admiral Halon aboard the Endeavor. I'll send you my terms of surrender in a moment."

Dean made a sign and Kon cut the connection. "Nellie, how's your aim?"

"I can give you one shot right down the pipe, Dee, then it's nap time."

"Do it, super woman. Make a hole for me."

Nellie focused for a few minutes. The Admiral was just hailing them when flaming witchfire shot from the gun port and sliced through three ships. As she slumped in her chair, Leen appeared and took the girl in her arms, softly chanting and smiling. A moment later Nellie sighed and sat up again. She stood and Leen helped her from the bridge.

Deann grinned. "Comms, hail them."

"Go ahead, Chieftain."

"Attention RIM ships. Is there anybody still alive over there?"

"Temon aboard the Seton. May I ask what that weapon was?"

"It was me," said Nellie, as she stepped in front of the screen. She was in scarlet robes with flames dancing around her form. "I'm Nellie, The Red Witch of Nova, and that was a sample of what I plan to do to you if you don't turn around and get the hell out of Nova territory." She turned and walked away. Leen caught her as she slumped again.

Deann stepped in front of the screen. "Actually, Temon, that weapon was witchfire. Pretty impressive, isn't it? You see, normally Nellie would be happy to let me deal with this sort of thing, but we've been in space a long time and she's in a hurry to get home to her kids. So, the problem here is, we have to clear you out of our territory. If you go back, we can go home and have done with the whole thing. If you put up a fight, Nellie will walk through your forces like a wildfire through dry grain."

"Will you give me time to confer with the other captains?"

"You get ten minutes then I bring this ship into that hole Red Nellie just blasted through your ranks until I find live ships, and then she'll do it again."

"Understood."

"Oh, Temon, I should tell you. Even if you somehow manage to get past me and reach Arcalian space, the king and his armada are waiting for you there. Not Goro the Usurper, but King Borad himself."

"Thank you, I think." Two minutes later he was back. "Seton calling the Novans."

"This Deann of Red Nova aboard the Raptor. What's your decision?"

"We'll leave and thank you for our lives."

"All right, Temon, send them out, but you stay here for a minute."

"Understood."

"Sensors?"

"Looks like they're leaving, Chieftain," said Tanie. "Several ships are moving away slowly. One is staying steady."

Deann nodded. "Still there, Temon?"

"I'm here. What are your terms of surrender?"

"First, tell me how many ships came in this pathway with you?"

"One hundred ships entered the Gap together. We lost nearly half that to the Gap before we encountered your people."

"How many do you have left?"

"Eighteen are functional," he replied with a sigh.

"All right, Temon, I need you to carry messages to the company for me."

"We're not to be held hostage?"

"Pay close attention now. Nova Clan doesn't take hostages. We don't take prisoners, and we never surrender. The Gap is our territory, and we defend it. We patrol it regularly. If you wish to pass through the Gap you fly under Novan escort. If you're found in the Gap without said escort you are considered an enemy and will be killed. These are the rules. Sector Nine knows them and abides by them. I expect the company to do so as well. This is the last time I let anybody walk back out of the Gap alive. Do you fully understand the rules?"

"Understood and recorded. Deann of Red Nova, may I ask a favor?"

"Speak."

"A few of these disabled ships have survivors on them. May I pick them up before I leave?"

"Do it quickly. We'll be watching." She signaled for Kon to cut the connection then turned to where Nellie was leaning against Leen. "What's holding you together, girl?"

"Leen is," replied Nellie. "Actually, Dee, it didn't drain me as badly this time. I think I'm getting better at it. I just need some practice."

"Nellie, you're the best, and sometimes you scare me. Tanie, what's going on over there?"

"That ship has picked up a number of small fighters and now they're pulling away, heading back to imperial space."

"And that's what I wanted to hear, people. Stand down battle stations. We'll hang around here until we're sure they're gone then we'll go find the family."

Putting it Together

They found the family near the edge of the Gap. The Warbird plus Zemma's two ships were headed back in at full burn. "Encroaching ships, you are entering Nova Territory. Power down and identify."

"This is the Warbird. Dee you nut, is everything all right?"

"It's over, Chella. The party's over and the uninvited guests have gone home. Lock up with us now, we want you back on this ship with us. Zemma, you there?"

"Right here, Deann."

"Your folks all right? Your ships still in one piece?"

"We're all right. I'm not happy about all those scratches on my new shiny ship, but what can you do?"

"I can get you a better one. Zemma, we're all gathering at King Borad's hunting lodge planet. I'd like you to be there for the celebration. You've earned it."

"Well, that sounds like fun, Deann, but ..."

"It's not a trap, Zemma. You pulled Chella out of the fire, helped us preserve Novan territory, and you've played straight with me. I owe you and I swear, if anybody tries anything they'll have me to deal with. Bring your people to the party. We'll feed them until they split, and we'll send our magic healers over to make sure everybody is on top of their game. Come on, you know you want to."

"Well, I suppose. Michella did talk the king out of hanging me from the nose cone of his ship. All right, we'll come to the party. How soon can I get those healers?"

"Zemma, talk to me."

"We've got some folks in bad shape, Deann. We do what we can for them when we cut them loose from the slavers, but we've never had a real healer with us."

"Comet, Warbird, put your healers on small fighters and send them over to Zemmas ships. Once they're aboard we head back to the hunting lodge, three quarter speed."

"Understood, Chieftain."

Deann turned in her chair to see Chella in Dor's arms, hugging him tightly. She smiled and signaled for the comms to be cut. Michella hugged her fiercely in turn then shook a finger at Kon. He swallowed hard, but didn't look away. She broke into a grin then turned back and kissed Deann.

"None of that on the bridge, ladies," chided Dor. "Take it back to the cabin. Go on, out." he shooed them away then relaxed back in the captain's chair. "Comms, ship-to-ship."

"Ship-to-ship, aye. Go ahead, Captain."

"Warbird, are you unlocked?"

"We're clear, Raptor."

"All right fleet, form up. Zemma, move your ships in behind the Raptor. Warbird, on my right. Comet, rear guard. Keep an eye out for Tangle ships just in case."

"Understood," came Quint's voice.

"Fleet, ahead three quarter speed."

———— ◉ ————

THEY ARRIVED TO FIND the king had sent most of his ships away, keeping only ten for escort. He joined them as they returned to the hunting lodge. There they found the clan chieftains and the viceroy, but most of the huge armadas had gone home. The viceroy, clan chieftains, and the king all wanted a meeting of the minds.

Dusk was falling, the fires were crackling, and meat was cooking on the spits when Arlessa called Deann to her. Deann came with Dor,

Michella, Nellie, and Zemma. Deann approached and knelt before the tall smiling woman in the flowing robes. "You called for me, Lady?"

"I did, Deann. Rise. It is good to see you still answer the call of the Temple."

"Lady, I ..."

"Hush now, Deann. I'm teasing you. Relax. We've called you here because Micha has something he wants to tell you."

"Oh no you don't, Mister," said Deann, rounding on him. "I know what you're up to."

"Dee, listen to me now," he said, smiling gently. "Hear me, all of you. Events have gone well beyond my control lately, as they too often do. In the beginning I appointed myself Lessa's protector. I acquired a crew and we continued to serve the high priestess. People, that's all I've ever been, the captain of Lady Arlessa's guard. That's taken me many places I'd rather not go, but it's been a good life.

"Recently I became a clan chieftain, not a task I'm cut out for." Deann started to speak, but Michella hushed her. "I've done my best for this new clan, but I'm a farmer and a reluctant warrior, not a clan leader.

"Deep within the Gap is a single planet that's good for farming and Novans are welcome there. Lady Arlessa wants to build a temple there for all Novans. As her guardian, I need to be there as does my crew. We can't do that and patrol the Gap at the same time.

"Some of you may know the story of Red Nova. For those of you who don't, you need only know, Red Nova is far more adept at defending our territory. You all need to know that over a thousand ships entered the Gap. Deann of Red Nova organized and led the defense of the Gap and not one single enemy ship got through to Sector Nine space. Neither did we lose a single ship to the enemy.

"I've been trying to convince Deann to take my place as chieftain of all Novans. I've asked Lady Arlessa to declare it so."

"And I do so declare," said Arlessa, a bright smile on her face. "Deann, will you accept this, or will you now abandon us to our fate? Please accept it. This gives Novans a home world, a temple, schools, and farms, a place to be instead of nomads. All Nova needs you. Please say yes."

Deann started to protest, but Michella and Dor both stepped in front of her, imploring her. "Dee, this is the only way, you know it is," said Dor.

"Dor's right, lover, you know he is," agreed Michella. "It's the only way to prevent what happened in his timeline."

Deann sighed and nodded. She looked around and saw all the chieftains, the viceroy, and the king all watching her closely. She stepped forward and spoke in a clear ringing voice, slightly enhanced by a smiling Arlessa. "If this is truly your wish, I accept. A number of years ago, less than two in your time, but closer to nine for me, I stumbled upon Red Nova. They spoke of a time when Arcalia fell, the clans were destroyed utterly, and so was Nova. They were all that remained of Sector Nine.

"I vowed to prevent that from happening in our timeline and I believe I've done so. King Borad still lives, Sega Clan has a new chieftain, and the people of Sector Nine are aware. That was all I hoped to do and more. My next and final task was to find a way to fit my Red Novans into Nova as a whole.

"I'll need some things, from all of you, to make this work."

"What do you need, Deann?" asked Arlessa.

"First, I'll need full acceptance from the other clan chieftains."

"Done," said Harral as she rose to her feet. She looked at the rest of the chieftains, but they all agreed. "Done," she repeated. "What else?"

"No more than you have already done," replied Deann. "You all came to back us up, yet you respected our territory. No more than this do I ask of the clans."

"No, but you're going to pillage my storehouses, aren't you," asked King Borad, a wide grin on his face. "I suppose you'll rob me of ships too." There was a great round of laughter at that.

"That and more, Sire," replied Deann.

"More? By all the stars, you're serious, aren't you? What else do you need, Deann. Name it and if I can make it happen, I will."

"Sire, this woman is known to many of you as Zemma the Bloody. Be it known to one and all, Zemma came running to the rescue of Nova Clan in the Gap and she fought as hard as any of us. I want you to issue a full pardon for her and her crews on condition she gives up pirating and joins Nova Clan."

"What???"

"Take the deal, Zemma," said Deann. "Think about it, a safe home world for your people, better ships to fly, ..."

"Deann, why?"

"Well, Micha's quitting to go farming. I'll need more ships and savages to captain them if I'm going to keep the Gap under control." She was grinning now. "Do it, Zemma. Help me keep our people flying free." Zemma nodded, unwilling to trust her voice.

"Sire?" asked Deann.

"Done then. What else do you need?"

"Supplies, as you have already agreed to do before. I'll also need teachers."

"Teachers?"

"Novans are tough fighters. Warriors without equal. I want them to be as strong in mind as they are in body. We have teachers now, but from time to time we may ask for some expertise in the arts or sciences, things like that."

"Done, Deann. You have only to ask, you know this."

"Thank you, Sire. You're a generous man and I do appreciate it. Now, there's just the basic rules about the Gap. You can visit, or pass through, but we need to know you're coming, and you'll need a Novan escort through. No escort, you're considered an enemy and will be dealt with accordingly. If this is acceptable to everybody then we're all good."

The meeting broke up then and everybody went back to feasting and storytelling. All the clans wanted to hear about Red Nova and Deann. She was just listening, Michella and Dor beside her, snuggled up. Her heart was full, and she was smiling, even though her mind was racing through the reorganizing of the Novans. Micha would take his original crew, plus anybody else who wanted to go back to farming, but some would stay in the air, she had Zemma's crew to blend into the mix, plus she would soon have new superior ships. Best of all, she could feel new life stirring inside her. Number three was inbound.

———— ◉ ————

IN THE DAYS AND YEARS that followed, Deann negotiated with the Fellie and brought them into the clan as well. The temple was built, farms established, but the training went on, the ships flew the patrols, and slowly enterprising pirates and entrepreneurs on both sides of the Gap learned to stay out. Trade continued to flow through, schools flourished, and the clan grew. That was how it all began.

———— ◉ ————

The End ... or is it?

———— ◉ ————

ABOUT THE AUTHOR:

Prudence MacLeod is a spiritual seeker, dog trainer, Reiki Master, interior designer, and personal trainer who has turned her hand to writing. She is an avid chess player and has recently become addicted to World of Warcraft.

In her own words, "I have roamed far and wide for over seventy years in this realm, and I have seen much; some I wish I had not, and a great deal that I would love to see again. Some days I feel like

Bilbo Baggins, for I have been there and come back again. No, I haven't written a book about my wanderings, but much that I have experienced, observed, learned, surmised, or imagined, is woven into the tales I have written. I do hope you enjoy them."

And now a peek at another story:

Lady Blue

by

Prudence MacLeod
Musings

IMAGINE WHAT MIGHT happen if the least powerful of us all was suddenly imbued with powers beyond imagining. They say that with great power comes great responsibility. How many of us could really live up to that responsibility, or would we all fall to the temptation of using that power for our own gain? Would we crumble under the weight of the responsibility, or would we rise to the challenge? Who can say for sure what they will do in any given circumstance, unless they have been thrown into that circumstance?

Perhaps Penny Preston might answer that for you, if by chance you might cross her path one day. According to the records, Penny disappeared many years ago, although, from time to time someone will admit to having seen her. Maybe former FBI agent Tara Montrose might help you find her, that is, if you can locate Tara. She seems to have...

A Cry for Help

Penny Preston's life was not one you might envy. Unwanted and abandoned by her father, emotionally abused by her alcoholic mother, barely tolerated by a series of her mother's boyfriends, Penny nonetheless managed to survive into high school. At just sixteen years of age, fifty pounds overweight with a bad complexion, and poor clothing, Penny had been dubbed Pee-Pee by her school mates.

The emotional abuse she suffered at home was nothing to what her peers put her through each and every day at school. Penny's blessing, and her curse, was her grades, which had earned a special scholarship to an upscale private school for her. Penny Preston was smart, way too smart to fit in with those she desperately wanted to fit in with.

Her grades and her love of history had, however, managed to win her a spot on the overseas class trip. Penny's mother certainly could not have afforded to send her, but her lifetime straight A average caused a local business to sponsor her.

This too had been a blessing and a curse. Penny had a mad crush on Brad Thatcher, the school super athlete, and everybody knew it. The blessing for Penny was that Brad was on the trip too. The curse was that she was the only poor kid there, and thus she had been singled out for still more abuse by her peers.

The trip had gone from bad to worse for Penny, and eventually it brought her to a sorry pass. She lay sobbing her heart out at the bottom of a mud slide, somewhere in the far reaches of the Scottish Highlands, a slide that she could not climb back up.

How had she come to be there? It's not so hard to guess really. She'd been mooning over Brad Thatcher and not watching her footing. One of the other girls tripped her, and she fell down a steep hill. The other girl had not even bothered to see how far she had fallen.

As Penny fell, she grabbed at the turf, but it gave way and turned into a fair landslide, eventually depositing her unconscious body beside a great slab of freshly uncovered stone. She was not missed until after the group reached the hotel later that evening.

The others were long gone, and it was dark when Penny regained consciousness with a pounding headache. She tried to climb back up to the foot path, but her leg was hurt, and the fresh mud kept slipping away from her feet. Penny called and called, but no one answered. She was thousands of miles from home, lost, hurt, terrified, cold, and miserable. She lay her bruised cheek against the hard stone slab and let a long incomprehensible wail of heartbreaking anguish escape her battered lips.

"Mooorrrraaaaaagggggghhhhhhhaaaaaa..."

By some strange inexplicable quirk of fate, Penny's wail awakened something that had slept for long ages. She was startled out of her misery by the sense of a vast presence near her. Penny stopped crying and shrank away from the stone as that unknown presence probed at her mind.

There was a clear demanding question, but Penny couldn't understand the language. Suddenly the presence vanished as quickly as it had arrived, leaving Penny alone with her misery, and feeling strangely empty inside. A few moments later the presence returned, and the sorrow it carried was so great, even Penny could not grasp the measure of it.

Again the presence invaded Penny's mind, probing, searching, demanding, until it seemed satisfied, and sadly withdrew from her. *"You are not of the bloodline,"* sighed a voice in her mind. *"Why did you awaken me to such a world, to such a fate?"*

"I... I didn't. At least I didn't mean to. Who are you? What are you? What is the bloodline? How did I awaken you?"

"Easy child, slowly now." There was a trace of amusement in that soft sighing voice, and the well of sorrow seemed to pull back a bit. *"I am Moragah. Long ages past my people dwelt here in this place. That stone against which you rest, was an altar they built to me. Long did we dwell together in harmony and peace, but eventually others came and brought their wars with them.*

"The people of the bloodline were too few, and, even with my help, they were still driven from these lands, scattered to the four winds, where they turned to other gods, other ways. My altar was cast down, buried, and so I slept, awaiting the return of even a single member of the true bloodline.

"As you touched the stone and called to me, I awakened, rejoicing. The folk had returned and rebuilt the ancient altar. I arose from the long sleep and came to you, but the altar is still broken, and you are not of the bloodline, so I sought them elsewhere. Alas, they are all gone."

The well of sorrow returned and threatened to swallow Penny whole. She lost all awareness of her own misery, as an up-swell of compassion for this bereft being filled her soul. "What happened to them?" she asked.

"They all died out, child, hundreds of generations ago it must have been. There is not a single trace of them anywhere in the whole wide world. Ah, to awaken to such news; better I had slept forever. At least there I still have them in my dreams." Penny didn't respond, she just quietly wished the being was solid, so she could give it a hug.

A soft chuckle escaped the presence and the sorrow pulled back again. *"Yes child, a hug is exactly what we both need right now. Tell me, how did you manage to awaken me?"*

"I don't know. I didn't mean to. I just leaned on this rock and cried."

"That wail of sorrow from your lips was close enough to the sound of my name to call me forth," chuckled the voice. *"Add to that the fact that you were touching the sacred spiral on the altar stone, and it was enough."*

"What will you do now?" Penny asked.

"What can I do? I am a goddess without a people to serve, or to serve her. They are gone, and even I cannot call them back. I am alone now. Perhaps, if I am lucky, I will be able to regain the long sleep, and rest forever."

"You mean die? You can't do that. You're a god for crying out loud. Up until this moment I wasn't sure that such a thing even existed."

"Truly? Is your own god no help to you, Penny Preston?"

"Look at me, for pity's sake. Look at the mess I'm in. What do you think?"

Again there was that rich chuckle in her mind. *"A fine pair we are, Penny Preston. A goddess without a priestess, and a human without a god. Perhaps there was a purpose to my awakening at that."*

"What do you mean?" Penny sounded a bit suspicious.

"I propose that we join forces, Penny. We each seem to have what the other needs."

"Wait a minute now." Penny pressed herself tightly against the huge altar stone. "You said priestess. I'm won't have to run around naked, chanting under the full moon will I? I don't want to end up in a rubber room."

"Penny, there is much I need to know about the world as it is today. May I explore your memories?"

"Will it hurt?"

"No, I swear it will not hurt."

"Well, okay, I guess..." The words were barely past her lips when every thought, every memory she had was suddenly invaded, explored, then released. For just a moment Penny Preston had merged thoughts with a goddess, and she was changed forever. As Moragah withdrew from Penny she left her a small gift; something Penny had not known before in her short lifetime; a true sense of self-worth. "Wow," she breathed, as she sensed herself alone in her own body again.

"I believe that, for this world, I will need a new kind of ritual for you to practice."

"What do you mean?"

"The old rituals are gone, Penny, vanished along with the people I designed them for. I will ask three things of you, Penny Preston, and I will return the favor to you."

"What are the three things?"

"The priestesses of old were warrior women, Penny, defenders of the weak. I will ask the same of you, but I will also give you the tools to accomplish the task. The priestesses of old honored me each day, and I will ask the same of you, but I will grant you the choice of how that is to be done."

"Okay, so far so good. Now what is the third thing?"

"Each of the chosen women was possessed of my spirit. I was always with them, sharing their thoughts, sharing their experiences. I was their goddess of protection, and of wisdom. I gave them the power to protect themselves, as well as others, and I shared what wisdom I could with them. It would be the same for you, Penny."

"Can you show me what that would be like?"

"It would be just as it is at this moment. We are now sharing thoughts and experiences. It would be as it is now. So, are you up for an adventure into the unknown with me?"

"As weird as this all is, I'm ready," sighed Penny. "You're the first I've ever known to speak to me with genuine respect, and you're the first I've found who is more alone than I am. I just hope I'm not dreaming this.

"Tell me, what did you mean, the tools for the task?"

"They are already in your mind, Penny. They come from your own mythology about the world you live in; Cat Woman, Spiderman, Rogue, feral mutants, Storm, Buffy the Slayer, they all have the tools for their tasks, and so shall you."

"So you're going to give me super power? I'll be like Buffy?"

"Something like that, yes. You shall have many abilities that you do not now possess."

"Okay, I'm game. What do I do now?"

"Take a deep breath and release yourself completely to me." Penny did as she was bid, then a soul wrenching tormented scream was torn from her lips, as every cell in her body seemed to burst into flame. It was over in a heartbeat, but it left her gasping for breath.

"Dear god that hurt. Why didn't you warn me?"

"Please forgive me, dear priestess. I guess I'm a bit rusty. In the old days a girl knew what she was in for, and she was ready. I will try to be more careful in future."

"Right, well, right now we have another problem."

"Which is?"

"I'm stuck down here. If you don't want your new priestess to die of exposure, you'd better do something about it."

"And so to work," chuckled Moragah. *"Rest now my daughter, while I arrange our escape."*

"Moragah, what tools did you give me?" asked Penny, as she settled down against the huge altar stone.

"I gave you the skills of old," came the soft reply. *"And a few I chose from some of your own heroes. It will be your task, in the upcoming days, to discover them for yourself. However, you already had the greatest gift of all."*

"I did? What was that?"

"Your natural intelligence, Penny. It is a priceless gift." Penny felt the presence of Moragah withdraw slightly from her then, and she huddled against the stone, trying to commit the symbol carved thereon to memory. Fatigue claimed her and she slipped into a deep and restful sleep. The next sound she heard was someone calling her name.

Don't miss out!

Visit the website below and you can sign up to receive emails whenever Prudence MacLeod publishes a new book. There's no charge and no obligation.

https://books2read.com/r/B-A-ZKBBB-LDURC

BOOKS 2 READ

Connecting independent readers to independent writers.

Also by Prudence MacLeod

Forgotten Worlds
Suvi
Echo of the Past
Survivors
Ship
Fleet
Unite
IGEN
T.E.N.

Nova series
Novan Witch
Assassin of Nova
Beyond Nova
Claimstake
Red Nova

Watch for more at https://www.prudencemacleod.com/.

Telling a story is like knitting a sweater. Start with a ball of possibilities, pull out one small thread and begin. With luck and patience you will create something quite wonderful.

About the Author

On a far off windswept island Jennifer Crandall sits with her dogs and cats creating fantastic stories for all to enjoy. She publishes as JL Crandall, Prudence MacLeod, and Jenni Leigh.

Read more at https://www.prudencemacleod.com/.

www.ingramcontent.com/pod-product-compliance
Lightning Source LLC
Chambersburg PA
CBHW020940180626
46814CB00003B/877